Geoff Ni

THE KNOT GARDEN

sceptre

British Library C.I.P.

Nicholson, Geoff, *1953–*
  The knot garden.
  I. Title
  823′.914 [F]

  ISBN 0-340-51599-6

Printed and bound in Great Britain for Hodder and Stoughton Paperbacks, a division of Hodder and Stoughton Ltd., Mill Road, Dunton Green, Sevenoaks, Kent TN13 2YA. (Editorial Office: 47 Bedford Square, London WC1B 3DP) by Cox and Wyman Ltd., Reading, Berks.

—THE—
KNOT
GARDEN

I mean to say, how could it have been anything other than suicide? There he was sitting up in bed wearing silk pyjamas, the telly was on, the curtains were drawn even though it was a nice spring afternoon, lovely for March, and the room wasn't even locked. It was all very tidy and there he was, in bed watching television, only he was dead. I mean, there was a whisky bottle on the bedside cabinet, and an empty bottle of sleeping pills. Well, the whisky could have killed him on its own if he could have kept it down, but with the pills as well there didn't seem to be much doubt about it.

I had a bit of a root around. It was all pretty well in order, clothes hung up all nice and tidy, no mess. You should see some of the rooms I have to go into, turns your stomach. And there was a small suitcase on the dressing table. I opened the case. There were a few things in it, just personal effects, nothing worth bothering about. I put the lid down again, fastened the clasps. I turned to the assistant manager who was with me and I said, 'Looks like an open and shut case.'

He didn't get it. He was looking a bit green at the time. I don't reckon he'd ever seen a stiff before. I don't reckon he'd seen much of anything. Hotel managers – I don't know where they get them from. Most of them couldn't manage a fart in a baked bean factory.

It turns out this stiff is called Richard Wisden, and everybody runs around like I'm supposed to have heard of him, which I haven't. Turns out he's a gardener. I mean, come on, how many famous gardeners have *you* heard of? Turns out he's on the telly a bit, runs a design firm, written a couple of books. Big bleeding deal. So it's all got to be kept quiet and kept out of the papers. That's what they tell me and they keep telling me, all of them keep telling me, the manager, the Old Bill, the PR girl, the doctor, everybody and his uncle. I mean what do they think I'm going to do? Stand outside selling tickets, 'Step this way and see the famous stiff, two quid a shot'? I mean what do they think I am? An arsehole or what?

So I kept my mouth shut. I mean who would I tell? None of my business really, is it? I'm only head of security. I'm only the bloody house detective.

So, to cut a long story short, a week later I'm sitting in my office, well I call it an office, it's more a phone booth with shelves, and there's a knock on the door and this bird walks in. Well, there's not enough room in there for two people to breathe so it's just as well that this bird takes your breath away, which is what she does. She must have been early thirties, blonde, a dark suntan even though it's only March, and not enough clothes.

'I'm Libby Wisden,' she said, as though that was supposed to mean something. But you know, a week's a long time in this game and I never was much good with names, and I wasn't supposed to know anything about it anyway. Eventually I tied in the name as being the same as the bloke who'd topped himself in the hotel. Now Libby Wisden looked the kind of woman I'd be prepared to keep on living for, but then again that might mean she was the kind some poor sod might be prepared to do himself in for. Either way you wouldn't have picked her out as a grieving widow.

She sat down without being asked, which was probably just as well because my manners are really crap sometimes.

'Mr Fantham,' she said, 'I understand you were the first person to see my husband after his death.'

Seemed a funny way of putting it but I said that was right – just me and the assistant manager, but he probably had his eyes closed.

'Did you notice anything unusual?' she asked.

Well, I didn't want to sound flippant but I tried to point out that we didn't find minor, dead television personalities in our rooms every day of the week, especially not Thursdays. I told her what I've told you, what I told the Old Bill, that the do-not-disturb sign hadn't moved for two or three days, there hadn't been any calls to room service, he didn't answer his phone. Either he was doing some serious meditating or he was having some bother. I told her about the whisky, the pills, the room being neat, the suitcase.

'Yes,' she said, 'they sent me the suitcase. Do you remember what was in it?'

As a matter of fact I did. I pride myself on the old memory. There was a camera, a pretty good one. It had film in it and there were thirteen pictures taken. There were a few little envelopes, which I worked out contained seeds, but there weren't any labels to tell you what they were. There was a map of Derbyshire and a kiddy's water-pistol in the shape of a ray-gun. Want to build a case on it? *She* did.

'Listen,' she said. 'My husband wasn't supposed to be in your hotel. He wasn't even supposed to be in London. He was supposed to be in Derbyshire making a knot garden.'

'A what?'

She didn't go into details, some sort of old-fashioned garden with herbs, which is what her husband specialised in. Nice work if you can get it.

'He said he was working on a knot garden, but he seems never to have arrived in Derbyshire. He set off. He told me that's where he was going, but he came to this hotel instead. He told me the house in Derbyshire didn't have a phone so I shouldn't expect a phone call from him. Then the phone call came from the police.'

'It must have been a shock,' I said, 'him doing himself in like that.'

'No, Mr Fantham. He didn't kill himself.'

'Not sure I'm with you.'

'I know that he didn't kill himself. It wasn't in his nature. I was his wife. I ought to know.'

Did she ought to know? Take my wife – yeah, somebody

did. I ought to have known about that. Husbands and wives always pride themselves on knowing each other. What's the big deal about knowing somebody?

'Are you saying it was an accident?' I asked.

'Possibly.'

'You've got to admit it's very careless to knock back a bottle of scotch and a bottle of sleeping pills by accident. Was he careless, your husband?'

She thought I was extracting the urine.

'Perhaps somebody else was involved,' she said. 'Foul play or whatever.'

'Somebody who stood over him with an axe and forced the drink and drugs down his throat.'

'I don't know what happened,' she said. 'I just know it wasn't suicide. It's your job to find out the details.'

Until then I'd thought my job was working in an overpriced establishment called the Hancock Hotel. However, she reached into her handbag and handed me an envelope with enough tenners in it to make me reconsider my job description.

'Give me a week of your time,' she said. 'Please. I don't know who else to turn to.'

When you're offering the rate of pay that she was there are all sorts of people you can turn to. You can look them up in yellow pages – surveillance, matrimonial, witnesses interviewed, industrial counter-espionage. Makes me want to throw up.

'Have you talked to the police about this?'

The expression that came on her face told me she didn't like the police any better than I did.

'They said I was overwrought. They said I should talk to my GP.'

Now I don't have the same technical back-up as the Metropolitan Police but if there's one thing Libby was not, it was overwrought. Maybe the grief hadn't hit her yet, but I had the feeling that it never would. It can't be easy for anybody when your wife or husband kills themself but why would you want to think there was foul play? One answer might all depend on how much you had him insured for. You can't claim life insurance on a suicide. Libby Wisden didn't look the type who enjoyed being strapped for cash.

'Did you and your husband get on?'

'Of course we "got on".'

'I mean, were you happily married?'

'What does "happy" mean?'

'I didn't know it took a lot of defining. Did you love him?'

'Is any of this relevant?'

I wasn't sure. Maybe not.

She said, 'We weren't well matched. We fought like cat and dog. We didn't like each other's friends. We weren't faithful to each other. But yes, we got on, we were happy, and yes, I loved him.'

I could understand that.

'When did you see him last?' I asked, coming on like a true detective.

'Last Monday morning. I drove him to the station – St Pancras.'

'But you didn't see him get on the train.'

'No.'

'He checked in to the Hancock on Monday afternoon. I found him dead on Thursday. I wonder what he was doing all that time. Sitting in his room watching the telly?'

'Not necessarily,' she said.

She handed me a packet of photographs. She told me they were from the film in the dead man's camera. The first half dozen were taken in the gardens of a stately home somewhere. I didn't recognise it but then I wouldn't – grass, paths, flowerbeds. They didn't look very special. The other seven did, though. They were taken in room 118 of the Hancock Hotel. The room wasn't nearly as tidy as when I'd last seen it. The bed was tangled. There were clothes strewn about, and on the carpet there was a girl wearing a studded belt and nothing else. It wouldn't have been so bad if I hadn't known her.

'She's called Trudy,' I said. 'At least that's what she's called this month. I've kicked her out of the hotel a couple of times. I could talk to her for you.'

Libby Wisden smiled. She looked great. It suited her. I had

11

another look at the envelope full of money. That didn't look bad either.

'Mind if I keep the photographs?' She didn't mind. 'You know this'll buy you a lot more than a week of my time if you want.'

She didn't say anything.

'And at the end of a week I might not have found out anything at all. Or I might have decided that he really did top himself.'

'Then I'll have wasted my money, but it's mine and I'm free to waste it any way I like.'

After she'd gone you could still smell her. It made my office almost bearable for a minute or so. I looked at the money again. Maybe I was getting a fetish for it. There was about five hundred quid. Nice work if you can get it. Only later did I have to start earning it.

The body is a machine. The body is an accident. It is a sack of chemicals. It is an electronic circuit. It is a map on which scars and symptoms reveal a more inner geography. The body is also a metaphor.

I had been Libby's GP for a long time. Her husband had briefly been a patient of mine, but he found he did not wish to be treated by a woman doctor. I did not really know Richard Wisden, which is not to say that I had not formed an opinion of him. He was boorish, arrogant, and not very bright. It therefore came as no surprise at all when he established himself as an occasional but very successful television personality.

It did, however, come as something of a surprise to learn that he had killed himself. It is sometimes gratifying to discover that one still has the capacity to be surprised by human nature and human action, and yes, Richard Wisden did not seem the 'type' to commit suicide, though I am well aware that there is no such thing as a type.

It did seem to me, however, that Richard's death would be one of the better things to have happened in Libby's recent life. She did not need his financial support, having her own flourishing career as a food expert and columnist, and having money of her own; and as far as I could glean she had not had the benefit of her husband's emotional support for a very long time. It would be overdramatic to say I thought Richard's death would bring Libby freedom, but at least it would give her the chance to find someone else. I am tempted to say someone better, but just as I know there is no such thing as a suicidal type, I tend to think there is no such thing as a good or better husband, just varying degrees of awfulness.

Libby rang me at the surgery and said she needed to talk. It seemed natural enough. I didn't know whether she had in mind a personal or professional meeting so I suggested she come to the surgery at the end of the working day, when I might proffer gin and tonics or medical expertise as the case demanded.

The moment she arrived I couldn't help remarking how well she looked, though I was quick to add that I knew this did not necessarily mean anything. She looked good and looking good is at least half the battle. Yes, physical beauty is largely accidental, but at least Libby knew how to use such accidents to her advantage. The rest of us have to make do with disguising the worst of the glaring deficiencies which nature has given us.

My offers of gin and doctorial skill were both spurned and Libby insisted on taking me out to dinner. One would never turn down such an invitation from someone so adept at dining out, and though it was very early we took a cab to an elegant if slightly poky restaurant in Kensington called the Morel, where the owner, a tall, camp, equally elegant black man, greeted Libby like a long-lost friend. We were shown to a corner table and we ordered camparis while perusing the menu.

It was only then that I enquired, rather leadenly, 'how she

was'. She said she was fine and I more or less believed her. She said she hadn't yet cried for Richard. I wondered if she would ever have any occasion to, but I said nothing. I was there to be a good listener.

She said, 'I knew Richard very well. Perhaps that surprises you. It would surprise a lot of people. I knew him well enough to know he wouldn't kill himself.'

I said, 'Is that because you don't want to believe it? And is that because it would mean you didn't know Richard as well as you'd like to think you did? You might think that indicates some failing in your marriage.'

She said, 'I was never under any illusion about the failings in my marriage.'

Yes, that was no doubt true. Their marriage looked nightmarish to an outsider, but that is how most marriages appear to me, and I have to admit that Libby seemed to find it serviceable enough.

She said, 'I'm not talking about some pop-psychological notion about not being able to "come to terms" with Richard's death. I'm saying, quite literally, that I don't think he killed himself.'

'You're saying it was an accident.'

She shook her head.

'Then you're saying somebody killed him.'

She said, 'I think that's what I'm saying.'

'Murder?'

'I thought that might interest you.'

She knew me better than I had realised. Yes, I'm one of those curious, not quite healthy souls who is interested in murder. It is an academic interest of course, not to say amateur. I am fascinated by the why rather than by the how or when. I am fascinated to know at what point the control mechanism fails, to know whether we all have the capacity to reach that point. Then, I have to admit, I enjoy the ironies of it all – the drooling madman identified by the traces of his saliva, the blood beneath the well-manicured fingernails, the sex-killer betrayed by his own semen. But I was not sure what any of this had to do with Libby's late and unlamented husband.

14

She said, 'He was supposed to be in Derbyshire building a knot garden for one of his old mistresses. I took him to the station, and the next thing I heard he was dead in some hotel by Paddington station. Why would he go there?'

I didn't want to say anything yet, but the fact that he'd gone to neutral territory seemed to speak in favour of suicide. Would she have found it less strange if he had done the deed in his own study, in some distant garden shed, in his mistress's bathroom?

She said, 'I want to know what he was doing in that hotel.'

'You say that as though you expect me to be able to tell you.'

The waiter came to take our order. We were not ready. We ordered more drinks.

Libby said, 'I've got something very difficult to ask you.'

'You only have to ask.'

'I want you to give me a week of your life.'

'Sorry?'

'To find out who killed Richard.'

I said, 'Libby, you need a detective, not an overworked, middle-aged doctor.'

She said, 'I have a detective, but I need you as well.'

'Seriously? You've actually hired a private detective?'

'Yes. He doesn't seem terribly good but he works in the hotel where Richard died, so at least he's on the spot. I think you have a much better chance of discovering something. You're a doctor. People talk to you.'

I was certainly prepared to give Libby a week of my life but in this case I was unsure what she was asking. If Richard had died in some spectacular or interesting way, or if he had been a somewhat more appealing human being, the project would have interested me much more. I had never wanted Richard dead exactly, but for Libby's sake it would have seemed a good thing if he had been silently and painlessly removed, like an appendix.

'I'll do what I can,' I said. 'I'll do anything you want. But where do I start?'

She handed me a slip of paper. She said, 'This is the address where Richard was supposed to be making the knot garden.'

It was, of course, a Derbyshire address. It would mean a long day's travelling. I would need to engage a locum. I would need to plead illness or family problems. But that was the least of what I was prepared to do for Libby.

I found Trudy in a cocktail-cum-wine bar three streets away. She looked expensive but approachable.

'You,' she said. 'You're not going to give me a hard time are you?'

I said, 'What kind of time did you give Richard Wisden?'

'What?'

'Long time? Short time? Swedish massage?'

'Who's Richard Wisden?'

'A punter, though you might have seen him on telly. He took this.'

I flipped a photograph on to the bar. It wasn't one of the ones taken at the stately home.

'I don't look bad, do I?'

'You look a lot better than Richard Wisden did.'

'Yeah. I heard about it. It was the day after he picked me up. At least he died happy.'

'You've got a high opinion of yourself.'

'It's justified.'

'Tell me about it.'

'You know, when he picked me up I couldn't help thinking I knew his face from somewhere.'

'What did he say to you?'

'What do you *think* he said? He asked how much.'

'Did he seem depressed? Did he seem like he was about to do himself in?'

'How should I know? The conversation was along the lines of undress, lie down, get on top, suck this. You know, I was just a whore as far as he was concerned. Was he depressed? Well, they often go a bit broody when they've finished, don't they?'

I had to take her word for it.

'And as for suicidal, well, aren't we all?'

'It's not enough, Trudy,' I said.

'Not enough for what?'

'Not enough to stop me telling the Filth that you were in on Wisden's death.'

'I wasn't in on anything. I did what he wanted. He got what he paid for. I went home, then he killed himself. I don't see any connection between me and it.'

Neither did I, but I said, 'How long do you reckon it would take to convince some cement-head down at Paddington nick that there wasn't any connection?'

'All right,' she said. 'I'll play ball, but I don't know what you want to know.'

'Did he talk about his wife?'

'No.'

'His work?'

'No.'

'Tell me about the pictures.'

'He said he wanted to take some pictures. I said that'd be an extra fifty quid.'

'Like I said, a high opinion.'

'It's called knowing what the market will take.'

I said I wanted her address. She gave me a card, 'Trudy, Young Model' and a phone number. She scribbled an address on it. There was no way of knowing whether or not it was real but it was the best she was offering at that moment.

'Don't make trouble for me, all right?' she said.

I shrugged.

'Don't make trouble and you can have a freebie. How about that?'

I told her not to be silly. There's no such thing as a freebie.

I went back to the Hancock Hotel. I took the pass key and went to room 118. It wasn't being used. They weren't going to use it again until they'd got a new bed. Yeah, this was a very high-class organisation I was working for.

I did my detective act in room 118. I searched the place, had a butcher's under the sink, in the cistern, under the carpet, behind the mirror, under the bed. I just got my hands dirty. I slouched on the bed. Sure, it was a depressing little room all right. You could kill yourself in a room like that without much problem. There wasn't anything there to remind you of the joys of living. I lay back on the bed and stared at the ceiling. It was papered with wood-chip. That needed replacing more than the bed. One of the edges where the sheets of paper meet had come unstuck and it was a bit tatty as though someone had been picking at it.

The next person who picked at it was me. Somebody had shoved something in betweeen the paper and the ceiling. There was a bulge about the size and shape of a car key and that's what I found – a car key. The ceiling was a funny place to have hidden it, not exactly inconspicuous. I wondered why the Old Bill hadn't found it, but I didn't wonder for very long.

The register didn't say that Wisden had a car with him, and although there were a few cars in the hotel car park that I didn't recognise, the key didn't fit any of them.

Since I knew Libby had dropped her husband at St Pancras I thought the key might belong to a hire car. Next morning I called in sick at work and did the rounds of the car-hire firms around St Pancras. They were an unhelpful bunch of stiffs. I mean, I thought my story wasn't bad. I told the truth about who I was and where I was from, and I asked if they'd lent out a car to anybody called Wisden, and whether they'd got a car missing, and maybe I could help them find it. I thought they'd have been interested in getting their car back. They weren't having any of it. It was well into the afternoon before I got my first kind word.

The place was called Vesta Car Hire. It looked a cheap operation, one that didn't do much business.

It was a converted corner shop with big plate-glass windows painted over white.

There was a skinny young half-Asian kid behind the desk. He was eating a Big Mac and reading *Marxism Today*. He had on a tee-shirt that had 'Don't go down to the woods today' printed on it. I didn't have high hopes but I started my spiel.

18

'Hello. My name's John Fantham. I'm in charge of security at the Hancock Hotel.'

The kid's eyes lit up and he put down the magazine and burger. You'd have thought I was the man from Littlewoods.

'The Hancock,' the kid said, 'that's where he died.'

'Who's that then?'

'Richard Wisden, of course.'

'How did you hear about that?'

'Papers.'

'Did it make *Marxism Today*?'

'He was great. Made great programmes.'

'You're the only fan of his I've met. Pity you're too late to get his autograph.'

'I've already got it.'

He pointed to the wall beside his desk. It had got safety notices and postcards and a map of London taped to it, and there was a square of paper with 'To Tony, Best wishes Richard Wisden' scrawled on it. He wrote big with a lot of curls.

'Are you Tony?'

'Yeah.'

'How did you get his autograph?'

'I asked him for it when he came in to hire a car. He was very kind, a real gentleman.'

'There aren't many of us left. When did he hire the car?'

'Last Monday. Why?'

'The Monday before he died.'

'I suppose.'

'Did you ever get the car back?'

'No. I think the boss is starting to get a little bit worried.'

'Who's your boss?'

'Nobody you'd know,' and he gave me a look that told me I wasn't going to find out, not then anyway.

'Did you talk much to Wisden?'

'I said how much I liked his programmes.'

'What did *he* say?'

'Thank you very much.'

'I don't suppose you know why he needed the car.'

Tony shrugged.

'How much of a fan were you, Tony?'

'Pretty good.'

'You don't get many teenage lads who are keen on gardening, do you?'

'I suppose not. It was just him. Just his charisma.'

I tried a very unlikely tactic. I took the packet of photographs from my pocket and spread out the half dozen pictures of the garden at the stately home.

'Recognise it?' I asked.

'Yes, it's Redlands. It appeared in one of his programmes.'

'Where is it, Derbyshire?'

'That's right. Hey, what are the other photographs you've got in there?'

'You wouldn't be interested, Tony.'

'Bet I would. Are they of the girl?'

'What girl?'

'The girl he was with.'

I picked out a picture of Trudy and showed it to him.

'That's her all right. Nice breasts.'

'I've seen better but I've been around more than you.'

'They're nice enough for me,' he insisted.

That was really about the full extent of the information I got out of Tony. He'd been a godsend, even if he wouldn't tell me who his boss was.

The whole thing was starting to smell like a tin of old cat food. If Wisden was really on his way to killing himself on Thursday, would he have spent Monday swanning about signing autographs and hiring a car? He checked in to the Hancock on Monday afternoon so if he'd hired a car he ought to have had it with him. Also he must, at the earliest, have met Trudy that same Monday morning, and not picked her up for the first time that Wednesday which is what she'd told me.

We entered his room because there hadn't been any signs of life for three days, but I suppose he could have left the do-not-disturb sign on the door and left the hotel without being seen. He could have gone anywhere he liked – even to a house called Redlands and taken some pictures of the gardens. But if he really wanted to go to Derbyshire why hadn't he gone by train as planned? Why sod about with some lame outfit like Vesta Car Hire? Maybe they tried harder. But there was no way of being sure he *had* been to Derbyshire. I mean, a few pictures in a camera don't mean much. They could have been in there for months.

On the one hand it all seemed easy, plenty of clues, a couple of people with information to give me. On the other hand none of it made any bleeding sense. I was going to have to have another little chat with my little friend Trudy, but that was going to have to wait till tomorrow. I'd got a real craving for a Big Mac.

It was a cool, bright morning when I set off for Derbyshire. A good morning for driving. The M1 was busy with drivers displaying the forms of death-wish that characterise modern, motorised man. I kept to the centre lane and listened to Tippett on the Panda's cassette player.

I do not know the Peak District well. I came off the motorway at Junction 29 and drove across country through places with not quite convincing names – Wadshelf, Curbar, Froggatt. The address I was looking for was to be found off a wooded B road, tucked beside a reservoir. The landscape was impressive. The house was called Woodbine Cottage. Richard Wisden's mistress was called Angelica.

I found the place with considerable difficulty, after numerous wrong turnings and several encounters with rather aloof locals who, probably deliberately, misdirected me. It had taken me four hours to make the journey. It was mid-afternoon.

To an optimistic estate agent Woodbine Cottage would have spoken eloquently of character, development potential, distinctiveness. To an unredeemed urbanite, like myself, it shrieked of leaking roofs, outbuildings full of rats, raging

21

woodworm, damp, and a crucial lack of central heating. I was not certain that I would know a woodbine if I saw one, but the garden, even to my untutored eyes, was clearly overgrown with nothing more appealing than weeds, grass, nettles and the occasional rogue wild flower. The site was quite large and on a steep slope. Now who was I to suggest that Richard Wisden was not sufficiently gifted and industrious to have turned the land into a finely wrought garden, bedecked with exotic herbs and formal delights? Suffice it to say, it would have been a Herculean task and it was clear he had not even begun.

It would have been easy enough to drive past and think that the cottage was deserted, but as I drew close it was possible to see a newish car parked beside the building and to see that the side door to the house was open. There was a child visible inside the house, a young boy aged ten or eleven. He watched me with all the suspicion I probably deserved. This was a lonely road and not a place, I would have thought, for a woman living alone with a child. She would need at least a dog, if not a shotgun.

I got out of my car and approached the house. I had contemplated various kinds of subterfuge to make my arrival seem less threatening but at last had decided that honesty, however threatening, would serve me best.

I opened the garden gate. The boy walked out to confront me.

He said, 'Who are you?'

I said, 'Dr Maureen Temple.'

'We're not poorly,' he said, but he was obviously somewhat impressed by the medical title.

'Is your mother in?'

That question seemed to create a problem. He had to consider his answer for some time, which gave me a moment to study him. Had he arrived at my surgery one morning he would have given me considerable cause for concern. He was far heavier than a healthy boy of ten or eleven should be. He moved too slowly and the eyes were too dim. Diet might be a factor, but there were other areas I should want to investigate.

He said, 'Yes, she's in, but I don't know if you can see her.'

'And why not?'

There was another long pause for thought, for the marshalling of words and ideas that seemed to elude the boy.

He said, 'She likes to lie down in the afternoon.'

'Let's not disturb her then. What's your name?'

'David.'

He said that very brightly, very promptly, as though he might have been practising and had finally mastered the trick.

'Shouldn't you be at school, David?'

That was an infinitely harder question to answer, although it too was perhaps one he had been often asked before. He did not answer.

'You don't like school?'

'No.'

'I don't blame you. Why don't you like it?'

He said, 'Boring.'

I said, 'Yes, it often is. Do you like living here?'

Another long pause until he said, 'It's all right.'

I asked, 'Do you have many visitors?'

It seemed he didn't understand that. I said, 'Do many people come to see you and your mother?'

He said, 'Yes,' then became silent and inert. It seemed I had asked the wrong question, or perhaps I had just asked too many and he was unaccustomed to so much mental activity. I didn't press him.

Then a voice behind me said, 'Who the hell are you?'

I turned. A woman was standing in the doorway. She was a big woman in a loose-fitting, flowered dress. The face was heavy and tired but had probably once been considered pretty. The hair was long but unwashed. The feet were bare. The hands were filthy. She was also quite obviously under the influence of drugs of some kind. I introduced myself.

'I still don't know who the hell you are.'

I said, 'I knew Richard. He was a patient of mine once. His wife still is.'

'Did Anderson send you?'

23

'Anderson?' I said.

She said, 'You'd better come in.'

The kitchen was dark but not dark enough to hide a range of festering pans and plates that lurked in the room. The radio was tuned to a pop music station and Angelica did not turn it off. I was offered a cup of tea and accepted it in the interests of politeness, but in the interests of hygiene I did not drink it. The boy wandered in and asked for a glass of orange squash. His mother instructed him to 'piss off and play'.

Angelica said, 'I suppose there's a will.'

I supposed there was, though I had never given the subject a moment's consideration.

'How much am I due?'

I assured her I had no idea but I imagined the proper authorities would be in touch with her if they deemed that necessary.

'So if you're not here about money, what are you here about?'

'Richard's wife asked me to come.'

Angelica said, 'Did she? Stuck-up cow. Why couldn't she come herself?'

I bristled. I said, 'She's far too upset.'

Angelica gave an intoxicated laugh.

I said, 'She wonders whether there were any unusual circumstances surrounding Richard's death. She wonders whether you might have any information.'

'Don't be bloody stupid. I haven't seen Richard for the best part of six months.'

'Well that's very interesting in itself, Angelica. You see Libby . . .'

'What a bloody stupid name.'

'Libby was told by Richard that he was coming to see you.'

'If she believed that she's an even sillier cow than I thought she was.'

I said, 'I quite understand your feelings of antagonism but I don't feel it's helping us very much.'

'That's because I don't *want* to help you very much. Look, I've had it up to here with Richard Wisden and his missus.

He was a hopeless little loser when I met him twelve years ago, out of work, penniless, and a crappy little womaniser. I happened to fall in love with him. Yes, I'm bloody stupid too. All I ever got out of Richard was that half-baked specimen you see in the garden, and the moment poor David appeared Richard was gone. Then a few years later he got famous, got rich, and got married to that cow; then he started wanting to see me again. And like a fool I agreed to see him, but I still didn't get anything out of him. Then a year or two ago he started getting big ideas about doing my garden for me. Well piss off, Richard, I said. That really is it. That's the last bloody straw. Here I am without a decent roof over my head, with wiring that's going to blow me up one of these days, without even a decent bit of stair carpet, and this silly bastard wants to make a knot garden for me.'

I found her anger perfectly understandable. I said, 'But he never did make a knot garden for you, did he?'

'That's really observant of you. He went on and on about it for a couple of years. I think he even did the design, though he never showed it to me, like it was supposed to be a surprise or something. I couldn't believe it. In the end I told him to stop pissing me about and just piss off. And he did.'

She started to laugh, but there were tears in with the laughter.

I said, 'So tell me, Angelica, why do you think Richard told his wife he was still seeing you? Why do you think he claimed to be making a knot garden when apparently he was doing no such thing?'

Angelica said, 'Because he was a lying bastard. He enjoyed telling lies so that nobody else knew what was going on. It never made any sense. I think he liked to confuse people. He thought it made him more interesting.'

I said, 'Do you think he was murdered?'

'What do you mean by that? How should I know? You're a doctor aren't you? Don't doctors know about these things? Don't they cut up the body and find out? What did it say on his death certificate?'

I said, 'There isn't a death certificate yet, and won't be till after the inquest, but there has been a post mortem and the pathologist's findings are entirely consistent with suicide.'

'So what's the problem?'

I said, 'Libby thinks otherwise.'

'How the hell would she know anything about it? She didn't know Richard. She didn't even know when he was lying and when he was telling the truth, and she didn't care so long as they still went to the right restaurants.'

'What did Richard lie to Libby about?'

'Oh you know, everything.'

The possibilities of Richard leading some sort of secret life that he kept from Libby flitted through my mind. I considered the basic building blocks of intrigue and mystery – violent crime, obsession, deviant sex, drug addiction, murder. They seemed a banal collection. Perhaps Richard had no secret life. Perhaps he just wanted to give the impression that he did.

I said, 'How much marijuana do you smoke?'

'As much as I can get.'

'Do you ever take anything stronger?'

'Mind your own damned business.'

'How do you afford it? Wouldn't it be better to spend some of that money on your son?'

'Oh, piss off, doctor.'

I accepted her reaction. I am no do-gooder. She paced the kitchen. She looked out of the window. While we had been talking a car had parked in front of the house. We had not heard it because of the radio. There was a man, large, smartly dressed but coarse featured. He was in the garden towards the rear of the cottage, talking to David, and he was attempting to open the boot of what I then took to be Angelica's car. She opened a corner cupboard. She may not have had a dog but she was certainly the owner of a shotgun. She loaded it and strode into the garden, giving every appearance of being about to use it.

Of course my students get younger every year, but from where I'm standing who doesn't? Not only the police but cricket umpires, newsreaders, wanted criminals, even Russian politicians.

All I can say is thank God I'm not a maths lecturer. They're supposed to have had all their ideas by the age of thirty. At least with the study of literature age does guarantee some advantage gained from the accumulation of experience; nothing to do with ideas, just the fact that I've read Proust, *Moby Dick*, *Don Quixote* and *War and Peace*. I've had the time and the opportunity to get through them all. My students haven't and they haven't. That's how I keep one step ahead while getting one step nearer the grave. I'm lucky if my students have read *Cider with Rosie* and *To Kill a Mocking Bird*.

In seminars, lectures and tutorials a sea of clean but empty faces ripples past me. They all seem to have good complexions, peculiar but pricey haircuts, and these days they even polish their shoes. The only ones I can remember are the lumpen misshapen ones. They only lodge in my memory by virtue of their big noses and speech impediments, and even then I don't remember their names.

So when there was a knock on my door and an extremely good-looking blonde woman in her early thirties walked in I couldn't be one hundred per cent certain that she wasn't one of my students. For all I knew I could have been teaching her Dryden. She had more poise and better clothes than most of the mature students but I couldn't be certain. But then she said, 'Hello Mr Rowntree, I've always admired your work', and I knew she had to be a stranger.

For my sins I once wrote a book of literary criticism called *The Fiction of the Hero*. It wasn't very good but it was

27

passable, and it became that very bizarre phenomenon – a fashionable book of lit crit. The real academics urinated on it from a great height, for its trendiness, its lack of rigour, its unquestioning acceptance of trendy ideas. Today it seems to me that they got it about right, but in those days I was an academic yobbo who was more than happy to do battle with a bunch of old eunuchs who considered Henry James to be the last word in modernity. The book acquired (oh God) cult status. Bright and beautiful young men and women started wanting to come to this university because this trendy young academic called Rowntree was teaching a course in Modernism here. My lectures were packed, dope was sometimes smoked. This trendy young academic was offered any number of firm young female bodies. He was also offered some firm young male bodies, but declined. It seems perfectly obvious to me from textual evidence that *The Fiction of the Hero* is the work of an eager heterosexual, but not all my students were spectacularly good at textual studies. I was also offered a number of soft young female minds, and I am proud to say that I declined the opportunity of moulding or carving them to my own specifications.

The book was published the best part of ten years ago now, and today it is not so much discredited as declared never to have existed; and I have published nothing since. Somewhere in the book I entertain the notion that every utterance is a blot on silence, and like a good Beckettian, in fact most unlike a good many of them, I have shut my face. I am delighted not to have fulfilled my early promise, but the book does sometimes come back to haunt me. I was once on a flight to Florence and the girl in the next seat was reading the book. It was the start of a very long relationship. Her name was Stella and I live with her still. I also occasionally get a letter from some mental incompetent in Wisconsin who writes to ask what I meant on page 176 when I used the word hegemony.

And then one day Libby Wisden arrived. She said she wanted to buy a week of my time. I said steady on, and made some coffee. She made a few remarks about what a lot of books I had in my office. I said she should see my house. She

28

said she'd read my book when it first came out, and after the usual nonsense about what was I working on these days (answer: nothing), I was expecting her to ask me to come and lecture to a group of Spanish-language students. But no. She said she wanted me to 'locate' her husband. I inevitably said she should contact the police; the missing persons department, if there is such a thing. Then she said her husband was dead and I wasn't sure if that was supposed to make locating him easier or harder. I contemplated ringing the porters' lodge and asking them to remove this insane woman, but then I thought I really ought to be able to deal with it myself.

She opened the shoulder bag she was carrying. I wondered if she was going to produce a bottle of acid, or even a gun, but no, this was England, this was a university campus, and instead she produced three hardback books and a scrapbook. She said these were her husband's complete works, and would I read them and tell her what they revealed about her husband. She obviously hadn't read my book very closely (there's a whole chunk where I pour scorn on the fallacy of gleaning anything about an author from his works), but somehow I found it in me to forgive her for that.

I looked at the three hardbacks. They were slim, which always bodes well, but they were about gardening, for God's sake. I said this. She said of course they were about gardening. Her late husband was a gardener. I had been imagining he was a frustrated writer. That I could have dealt with. I said she should talk with another gardener. She said she intended to but she wanted a literary opinion first. Then I suggested she might be better approaching a practising writer rather than a critic. She said that sounded like a good idea, could I recommend one? However, she made it clear that was to be as well as me, not instead of.

The books were entitled *The Happy Herbalist*, *Grand Designs*, and *A Turn around the Parsley Patch*. The scrapbook contained press cuttings. They were Richard Wisden's articles, generally culled from glossy magazines with colour photographs of plants, gardens and sometimes food.

She wondered if I'd need more than a week. I said that I was well aware that length was no indication of density or

29

difficulty, but I thought I could probably struggle through the texts in that amount of time if I wanted to, but I wasn't sure that I *did* want to.

She reached into her shoulder bag again and produced a wad of £20 notes. She said the money was mine whether I decided to do the work or not. I said wait a minute. I said all sorts of nonsense. Did she want to have lunch in the cafeteria? Surely there was more information she wanted to give me. Surely there were some things I ought to know about his life and death. To my considerable surprise, and partly to my relief, she assured me we were adopting a *nouveau roman* stance here, and she didn't want me to have any extraneous information. She wanted me to be alone, with only the texts for company. I found this very encouraging. She gave me a London phone number where she could be contacted. She thanked me. For some reason I thanked her in return. All I had to do now was read on.

When I got home with my Big Mac there was a gorilla standing in the middle of my living room. I mean he was wearing a suit and he smelled of after-shave, but he still had more in common with a gorilla than he did with most humans. A gorilla might have been a lot easier to reason with as well.

'What's your problem?' I said to him as I walked into my own flat.

'I haven't got a problem,' he said. He had an American accent. 'You're the one with the problem.'

I sat down on the settee in front of the coffee table and opened the bag that had the Big Mac and the large fries in it.

'While you're on your feet, John,' I said, 'there's a couple of cans of lager in the fridge. Run and get us one and you can have one yourself.'

He walked into the kitchen, well I call it a kitchen, it's really just a cubbyhole with a cooker. He got one can of lager out of the fridge, opened it and took a swig. Then he lit one of the burners on the gas cooker. I didn't know what that was all about.

'I wasn't all that bothered about a lager,' I said. 'Hey, are you here to put the frighteners on me?'

He nodded.

'I frighten very easily,' I said, which was absolutely true. 'Why don't we just say you've frightened me and then you can be on your way?'

'Don't start getting funny.'

'I wasn't being funny.'

'Oh.'

He took another drink from the can of lager, then emptied the rest of the contents all over my carpet.

'Oh, come on,' I said. 'You didn't need to do that.'

'Shut up,' he said.

I thought he meant it so I shut up. He scanned the room looking for things to break. I didn't have all that much. There was a stereo, he broke that; a clock, he broke that. There was a picture of me and my ex-wife and our daughter Diane when she was a baby. He picked it up and was about to break that too.

'You leave that alone, you fat bastard,' I said, which looking back on it was a mistake. He didn't like me calling him that. I saw the red balloons pop behind his eyes and I knew I was the next thing he was going to break.

I tried to make a run for it. I got halfway to the door before he smacked me on the back of the head. It was like being hit with a frozen leg of lamb. I fell over but that didn't matter. He picked me up again and dragged me into the kitchen. He turned up the lit gas, grabbed my right arm just below the elbow and held it so that my hand was six inches above the flame.

The gorilla said, 'Forget about this guy Wisden. Forget about that little whore in the hotel. Forget all about Vesta Car Hire. Okay?'

I said, 'Who's paying you, you fat bastard?' He moved my

arm so that the hand went down into the gas flame. He held it there for a while, not all that long, just long enough for it to start looking like a piece of overcooked bacon. Then he threw me back into the living room.

'That's all,' he said. 'It could have been a whole lot worse, couldn't it?'

'I'll see you again some time, friend,' I said, but I hoped I was wrong.

He left the flat. I ran my hand under the cold-water tap. I dialled for a taxi with my left hand and took myself off to a casualty department. The National Health, what a bad joke. You sit in a corridor for an hour till some doctor with a smarmy accent tells you you've burned your hand. I got out about nine. I went and had a double scotch and a pint. Then I got another cab, this time to the address that was on the card Trudy had given me. It was a mews house in Kensington, expensive, well above her bracket I'd have thought, but what did I know?

I leaned on the bell and started kicking the door just in case anybody thought I might go away if I was ignored. A middle-aged woman in a stage maid's uniform opened the door an inch. I shoved the door open, knocked her aside and went up into the house.

'You can't go in there,' the woman yelled.

'Watch me, darling.'

There was a bit of a party going on in the bedroom. Trudy was there, as naked as she had been in Wisden's snaps, and she was showing a good time to some little old geezer with a hump.

'Get rid of Quasimodo,' I said.

He went for his jacket. I didn't know if he was going for a knife or a packet of Kleenex, but I hit him anyway, just to be on the safe side. It was only with my left and it wasn't all that hard, but it seemed to get the job done. He bundled up his clothes and ran for it. I only hoped he hadn't paid for the session.

'For God's sake put something on,' I said to Trudy.

'Aren't you the butch one?'

'You didn't pick up Richard Wisden for the first time last Wednesday, did you?'

'Hey, that's good. Anyone would think you were a detective.'

It wasn't a bad line. Credit where credit's due.

'What's the story?'

'He phoned me, said he wanted to meet me first thing Monday morning. So I met him. We didn't have sex or anything.'

'You hired a car.'

'You've been busy.'

'What did he do with the car?'

'He didn't do anything with it. He hired it then he went to register at the Hancock. I was the one who drove the car.'

'Where?'

'To Derbyshire.'

'Why?'

'Because that's what he was paying me to do. He wanted me to take some pictures of Redlands. It's only open to the public on Mondays, though I could have got round that. Then I had to hand the car over to a woman.'

'Hand over?'

'I took it to where she lived, then she gave me a lift into Chesterfield and I caught the train back to London, gave Richard his camera, and that was it.'

'You've still got this woman's address?'

'Somewhere.'

'Find it.'

She scrabbled in her handbag and found a scrap of paper. I took it from her. It was an address in Derbyshire, some place called Woodbine Cottage. I couldn't see why anybody would want to call their house after a make of cigarettes.

I held up my bandaged hand and said, 'If you know who's responsible for this, you tell 'em it was a big mistake.'

Yeah, that's me all over – very hard with tarts and hunchbacks, not so hot with gorillas.

It was a bastard of a drive to Derbyshire. Changing gear was all right, but steering was a bit hairy. I set off early and stopped a couple of times on the way. In one of those

33

little supermarkets you get at the services where they sell magazines and toys I noticed they were selling pink, plastic water-pistols in the shape of a ray-gun, pretty much like the one I'd seen in Richard Wisden's suitcase. I don't know why but I bought one.

I got to this Woodbine place at about a quarter to two. God knows how anybody lived there. It looked like it should have been condemned years ago, and the garden could have been a training ground for jungle warfare. But the house was obviously lived in. There was a car parked outside with a doctor's sticker on it, and round the side I could see a much newer job. With a bit of luck my key was going to fit it.

I could see a kid playing in the garden. I got out of my car and waved him over. He was a funny, round little bugger. I couldn't decide whether he was only half there or whether he was playing dumb.

'Here,' I said, 'I've got something for you,' and I showed him the water-pistol. Talk about ingenuity, eh? He didn't seem very impressed but he took it when I offered it to him.

'What's your name?' I asked.

'David. What's yours?'

'You can call me John.'

'John who?'

'John Fantham.'

'Hello, Mr Fantham,' he said.

'Is that your car?' I asked, pointing at the car at the side of the house.

'Don't know,' he said.

'I've got a car just like that at home. See, I've got the key here. I wonder if this key will fit that car.'

I was hoping the kid really was as thick as he looked. He seemed to be going along with what I was saying, but he could have started screaming for his mother any second.

'Is this a game?' he asked.

'That's right.'

'Like *Transformers*?'

'A bit like that, yes.'

'All right then.'

I could see two women talking in the kitchen but I didn't

34

think they could see me, and they had Radio One playing so I hoped I was in with a chance of getting to the car without being seen. The key slid into the lock perfectly. The kid thought that was great. I didn't think it was too bad myself, and I was on the point of opening the boot when I looked up and saw the two women come running out of the house. One was small and middle-aged. The other was an Amazon with a shotgun.

'Hands up,' the Amazon said.

I felt like a pillock but I took the key out of the lock and I put my hands up.

Patients really do say to me, 'What are my chances, doctor?' People do actually sometimes say, 'Is there a doctor in the house?' For our part, members of our profession, some of them at least, really do say, 'Bring me lots of towels and hot water,' or even on occasions, 'Let me through, I'm a doctor.'

So, amid this scene of apparent rustic tranquillity, in the garden of Woodbine Cottage, I found myself in the company of a somewhat drug-affected woman who was pointing a shotgun at an unknown man who had apparently been trying to break into her car, who was now standing with his hands in the air. Then, to my eternal shame I'm afraid I found myself saying, 'Put away that gun, Angelica. Somebody might get hurt.'

If it is any excuse, the other actors in this scene were also overplaying their parts quite shamelessly. Angelica was speaking through clenched teeth and demanding to know who the intruder was, while the man himself seemed a little overfamiliar with the dialogue patterns of *film noir*. In addition, David was watching the events with a horrified fascination, his mouth hanging open in a slack smile.

At that moment I had no idea who the man was. He could have been a genuine car thief. He was clearly disturbed to be on the wrong end of a shotgun, yet he seemed commendably brave.

He said, 'Look, I've come rather a long way with this key,' and he showed that he was holding a car key in his raised right hand. 'Richard Wisden wanted me, or someone very like me, to find the key; and I'm rather keen to discover why. Also, people keep trying to inflict injuries upon me and I'd like to discover why that is as well. So I'm going to put my hands down and open the boot of this car and if you really intend to use that gun then I suppose you're going to shoot me.'

I had no idea where the key had come from, nor for that matter the car, but it did seem curious, and perhaps it should have seemed curious earlier, that Angelica was living in a ruin yet had a six-month-old car in her garden. I suspected that Angelica had every intention of using the shotgun; however, given the present state of her hand/eye co-ordination I thought it unlikely that she would hit her target. Events showed that I was more or less correct.

Angelica said, 'Are you police?'

The man said, 'Don't be silly,' and proceeded to open the boot.

'So who are you?'

'I'm from the Hancock Hotel.'

That made little impression on Angelica, but I realised at once that this was the detective in whom Libby had had rather little faith. She appeared to have done him an injustice.

He said to Angelica, 'Do you know what I'm going to find in this boot?'

The stuff of melodrama went through my imagination – a severed head, a bag of heroin, arms, explosives, missing documents. Then the tragedy happened. In retrospect it was a minor tragedy and only somewhat Aristotelian. The detective had opened the boot and had seen what was inside. Angelica was about to fire the shotgun.

She said something foolish like 'You asked for this', and David suddenly leapt between his mother and the detective.

36

He had a toy gun in his hand and he pointed it at Angelica. The gun went off – the real gun. The boy fell as though he had been kicked in the back. The detective dived for cover and I wrestled the shotgun away from Angelica before throwing it away as far as I could. We all three then ran to the boy. He was lying in what actually appeared to be a rather comfortable position, on his back, in the grass, and I am almost prepared to swear that he was smiling.

He had been hit in the calf. There was some blood but it was a superficial wound, no deep penetration, no splintering of the bone. Nevertheless he would not be running anywhere for some time, though I suspected he was the sort of boy who didn't do very much running.

The detective said, 'You a doctor then?'

I said that I was and this seemed to put everyone's mind, unnaturally, at ease.

I said, 'I can clean this here, but we'll need to get him to hospital.'

The detective said, 'You won't be needing me then.'

Angelica said, 'Nobody ever needed you in the first place. Did you get what you came scavenging for?'

He said, 'I never came scavenging.'

Frankly I found this sort of banter more than a little distasteful considering there was a wounded boy at our feet. I told them to be quiet, instructing Angelica to go into the house for cotton wool and disinfectant. I felt that neither item was likely to figure largely in this household but Angelica departed saying she would see what she could find.

David said, 'Am I going to pull through, doctor?'

I couldn't tell whether this was a genuine enquiry on his part or merely some sort of feeble-minded joke. I assured him he would survive and asked whether he had much pain.

He replied, 'I can take it, doc.'

I turned to the detective and said, 'It appears we're both on the same side. I'm a friend of Libby Wisden. I came here at her request.'

He said, 'I don't take sides.'

I said, 'If you've discovered something in that boot I think I'm entitled to know what it is.'

37

He said, 'You're not entitled to anything.'

He held up a large padded envelope. I asked what was inside it but did not receive the benefit of a reply. He started to walk from the scene, through the garden gate, to his car. He drove away.

I was left with the boy. I was furious and frustrated but I saw no way of pursuing the man and demanding to know what was in the envelope. Besides, I hoped Angelica might know. Once she was calm, once the boy was in hospital for the night, I had the feeling I might be able to get a great deal more information from Angelica. Trauma, sickness, the nearness of danger, these are the things that make people want to talk, to open their unremarkable hearts. Doctors are all too often recipients of this unsought and unwelcomed intimacy. This time I felt there was much to be gained by being a good listener for Angelica.

I took the books and scrapbook home with me that evening. I live with Stella in an expensive village set two and a half miles from the campus, on the estuary. The house has lots of small rooms. I sit at the top of the house reading, marking essays, never writing. Stella shuts herself away in a downstairs room and our paths do not cross unless we want them to.

After dinner I went to the top of the house, took the complete works of Richard Wisden and settled down for a preliminary reading. I hadn't told Stella about the arrival of Libby Wisden. It wasn't that I intended to keep anything back from her, and in fact Stella might have proved a valuable research assistant. She knew a little about gardens having been given sole charge of our small patch of lawn and our two flowerbeds. I had refused since adolescence to be seen dead with any garden implement in my hand.

The idea of spending an evening, much less a week of my life, leafing through gardening books, had a very limited appeal. But what the hell, getting through Pope had been no picnic either.

The first task was to determine the nature of the texts under discussion. Never mind the niceties of style, expression and psychoanalytic revelation, let's see what these texts actually *are*.

My heart sank when I immediately discovered that *The Happy Herbalist* was, oh spare me, the book of a television series. The jacket shows a short, portly, bearded man wearing a straw hat, standing in a field of lavender. The book has lots of photographs in black and white and colour, not much text, and what little text there is is broken up to look like a magazine, complete with cheery little headlines that ensure the reader never has to cope with more than one hundred and fifty words at a time. The headlines are things like: 'What is a Herb Anyway?' 'A Thyme of Beauty is a Joy Forever' 'Why Don't We Do It In The Woad?' The man does not seem to take himself very seriously which, in the book of a television series, is no bad thing.

In the words of the blurb writer, 'Television's happiest herbalist tells you all you need to know about growing, harvesting and using herbs. Whether you're planning a kitchen window box or an elaborate knot garden Richard Wisden will set you on the right garden path'.

I suppose blurb writers have to make a living the same as the rest of us. Two things struck me. First, Wisden has a tendency to lard his text with only partially relevant quotations, mostly from Shakespeare – 'I know a bank where the wild thyme blows', 'there's rosemary, that's for remembrance'; and secondly the book is dedicated 'To Angelica with love'. This had the feel of an interesting ambiguity – the name of a woman and the name of a herb. His wife was called Libby but Wisden might have given her a pet name, or it could have been his daughter (did he have a daughter?) his mother, his mistress or his cat. Bill Empson and I – two of a kind.

Grand Designs is a more scholarly work than *The Happy*

Herbalist though that is saying very little. It has fewer illustrations, more text, longer sentences and bigger words. That's what we mean by scholarly.

It is a book about garden design, especially about herb gardens and knot gardens, with some reference to parterres, topiary and mazes. The first chapter is called 'What is a herb?' and I assumed there would be some mileage in doing a 'compare and contrast' with the similarly titled section in *The Happy Herbalist*. In this second book Wisden seems to have a more interesting line in quotation. Such as:

> The even mead that erst brought sweetly forth
> The freckled cowslip, burnet and green clover,
> Wanting the scythe, all uncorrected, rank,
> Conceives by idleness; and nothing teems
> But hateful docks, rough thistles, kecksies, burs,
> Losing both beauty and utility.

Next day I would need to look into the various meanings of 'rank'.

The book seemed, I have to admit, an interesting one. You don't need to be George Steiner to know that world literature fairly teems with gardens, symbolic and otherwise. *Grand Designs* gives a quick listing of these. He talks at some length about Elizabethan gardens, knots, the history of herbalism, about Culpeper, Gertrude Jekyll, Vita Sackville-West (of course), and about the Tradescants.

I couldn't see that the book had an argument as such and it still seemed to be unmistakably a 'gift book', but even on this cursory glance there was the suggestion that somewhere in this text an interesting mind was trying to break through.

By contrast, the third book, *A Turn around the Parsley Patch*, showed an interesting mind that had taken a drink too many, been out in the sun too long and was starting to lose its grip. The title was odd and I suspected that it might contain some light sexual innuendo, confirmed, though not explained, by the appearance of the following quotation from Shakespeare: 'I knew a wench married in an afternoon as she went to the garden for some parsley to stuff a rabbit'.

The book contains an article called 'Herbs in Bondage', another called 'The Joys of Angelica', another describing a dirty weekend spent in the Lake District and discussing the connection between food, seasoning and seduction, a piece on the symbolism inherent in walled gardens, and an impenetrable-looking item of quasi-philosophy called 'A Contemplative Garden for 20th Century Man'.

I opened the scrapbook. There were articles with titles like '12 More Things to do with Chervil', there were some recipes using herbs, a few practical articles on herb growing, interviews with specialist gardeners, including one with a woman called Esther Howard whom Wisden describes as 'the woman who taught me all I know about herbs'. There was often a picture of Richard Wisden accompanying the articles. He would be sitting on an elaborately carved wooden seat, or almost submerged in a field of poppies, or working in his kitchen, usually wearing a loud, hand-knitted sweater.

I probably don't need to tell you that I had never heard of Richard Wisden until his wife entered my office. I'd certainly never seen him on television. The impression I got, and I realise this was not a wholly textual impression, was that Richard Wisden was a man trying to appear extrovert, flamboyant, lovably eccentric, but somehow he was trying too hard. If there was a real man to be found behind this self-presentation I wasn't sure I was going to find him in the curious selection of texts I had at my disposal; but at least by this time I was interested enough to want to try.

It was late when I'd finished my first reconnaissance of Richard Wisden's writings. I put the books and the money in a drawer of my desk. I thought of locking it but that seemed a little melodramatic.

Stella was watching television when I went downstairs. I asked if she'd ever heard of Richard Wisden. She thought for a second then said she had. She thought he was a great character and wasn't it a shame he'd died. He couldn't have been very old, though with the amount of weight he was carrying it wasn't all that surprising.

Then she said she'd met him once, though she wasn't sure you could really call it meeting. She'd seen him having a drink in a pub in Lambeth and she'd arranged things so that as he went to the bar to buy another round of drinks she was there as well. She told him she really enjoyed his programmes. He had seemed uncharacteristically embarrassed but had thanked her very much and that had been that.

We watched the late-night film, had a couple of big brandies. We often read before going to sleep but I had read enough for one evening. I wondered what sort of week I had ahead of me.

I mean, I felt a right berk standing there with my hands above my head. The bird with the shotgun was looking a bit glassy-eyed like she was on something. I didn't reckon she was going to shoot me but you can never be sure about these things. So we exchanged a few pleasantries about who I was and what I was doing there and all that, and I didn't give much away, but after a while I'd had enough. I was getting a bit pissed off with being threatened and heavied over. I decided to open the boot and be buggered.

I said, 'Look, I've come a long way with this key. Richard Wisden wanted me, or somebody like me, to find it, and I'm interested to know why. I'm also interested in why people want to keep damaging me, but maybe I've just got one of those faces. So the thing is, blossom, I'm going to put my hands down and I'm going to open the boot of this car; and if you've got the bottle to use that gun then I suppose I'm going to get shot at.'

It wasn't the best speech I'd ever made but at least it came from the heart. I took my hands down and she didn't shoot me. I put the key in the lock and she still didn't, but as I opened it I knew she'd made up her mind and she was going to do it.

42

I'd been keeping an eye on the kid all this time. He was a weird little nutter all right. I could see he was watching everything that was going on as though it was all a big game. It was like he felt left out and wanted to join in. He was holding the water-pistol as though he was covering a couple of suspects and just as the bird was about to fire the gun he leapt between us, held his water-pistol at arm's length and pointed it at her. I swear he yelled out 'Drop that gun', but I could have been mistaken, things were moving fast by then.

The shotgun went off and the kid keeled over. If he hadn't been in the way the shot would just have gone straight into the ground. On the other hand if the kid hadn't leapt in like that she might have taken her time and got a decent shot at me. The other woman grabbed the shotgun as soon as it was fired and tossed it out of harm's way, then all three of us ran across to see how the kid was. He was lying on the deck and he didn't look bad at all. The woman said she was a doctor and that was good enough for me. I wanted out of there. I'd got what I came for.

I hadn't expected to find the Crown Jewels in the boot of the hired car but even so I was a bit disappointed at what I *did* find. There wasn't anything in the boot except the spare wheel and a big Jiffy bag, and inside the Jiffy bag there were just a lot of smaller, sealed envelopes. Big deal. Even so I needed to get away from there and open some of those envelopes.

The little dyke tried giving me some crap about how she was a bosom pal of Libby Wisden's and we were both on the same side. I didn't know how many sides there were but I didn't intend hanging about to find out. I got into my car and drove off. Nobody was in any condition to stop me, and I didn't stop myself until I'd hit the motorway and come to the first lot of services.

I pulled into the car park and emptied out the Jiffy bag on to the passenger seat. There were thirteen envelopes – all more or less identical, thin, and all of them addressed to Libby. The handwriting looked pretty much like the autograph of Richard Wisden I'd seen at Vesta Car Hire. I've never had any qualms about opening other people's mail. Just as well. I

43

opened the first of the envelopes. There was a single sheet of white paper inside it and it read:

Dear Libby,
This is quite rational. Please give my love to Mother. I'm sorry but there was nothing left to do. Things went wrong too many times.
Richard

It was a bit of a stunner to be sitting there in the car park of a motorway service station and suddenly to find yourself reading somebody's suicide note. I opened the window, took a few deep breaths and read the letter again. It didn't exactly say much, did it? You'd have thought he might have sent it to his wife by post if he wanted her to get it, rather than leaving it in the boot of a hired car in the middle of Derbyshire. Still, maybe he wasn't as rational as he thought he was. I folded the letter, put it back in the envelope, and started to get very curious about what was in the other twelve. I opened the second one.

Dear Libby,
If you read his diary all will be explained.
R. W.
P. S. Especially the latter part.

Eh? Who was 'he'? What was the diary? And what kind of head-case puts a P. S. on a suicide note? I opened a third letter.

Dear Libby,
Unfortunately this is the only way to make good the frightful wrong I have done you, and the only way to wipe out my abject humiliation. I love you.
Richard.
You understand last night was only a comedy.

Yeah, it was all starting to sound like a comedy. What had happened 'last night', and which particular 'last night' was he referring to? What kind of wrong had he done her? I opened another letter.

Dear Libby,
Here's to my true love. O true apothecary!
Thy drugs are quick. Thus with a kiss I die.
Richard.

What's an apothecary? Who's his love? What did a kiss have to do with anything? And what's all this about drugs? And why's it written in this funny language? I opened a fifth letter.

Dear Libby,
I'm going out now. I may be some considerable time.
Richard

I mean, I never claimed to be very bright but I know when I'm being had. Nobody seriously writes thirteen suicide notes, puts them in thirteen separate envelopes, addresses each of them to his wife, puts them in a Jiffy bag, puts the bag in the boot of a hired car, gets a prostitute to drive them to the house of an old mistress of his in Derbyshire, then hides the key to the boot in the hotel room where he kills himself. Or do they?

I still had another eight envelopes to open but I didn't open them. I knew they were going to be full of the same sort of crap. If Richard Wisden was trying to tell somebody something he was going a bloody funny way about it and I couldn't keep up with him. I mean, I was still interested, I wanted to know what he was trying to tell me. It was just that he was dead and I couldn't catch his drift.

Then somebody tapped on the windscreen. I wasn't sure if it was trouble or not. I thought it was fuzz at first but it turned out to be two blokes in security guard uniforms. They opened the door of my car. I hadn't locked it, which was stupid of me. They told me to get out. I got out and I saw that one of them was wearing a badge that said Vesta Security.

One of them said, 'You're in serious bother, mate.'

'Oh piss off,' I said.

I knew it wasn't one of the great comebacks.

'Somebody told you to lay off. We meant it. This time we **mean it double.**'

45

He held out a gold necklace. It took me a second to realise what it was. I'd given it to my daughter Diane a couple of Christmases ago.

'We've got her,' he said. 'What we do with her all depends on you.'

I was supposed to be busy with Webster and Melville but I put them aside and retired to my study with a breakfast cup of Earl Grey and removed the works of Richard Wisden from my desk drawer.

I began by asking myself, just as Richard Wisden frequently did, 'What is a herb?' At first this seemed an easy enough question to answer – both for me and for Richard Wisden. In *The Happy Herbalist* he says that a herb is a useful plant, i.e. one used for its culinary, medicinal, cosmetic or fragrant qualities. By the time of *Grand Designs* this isn't enough of an answer. Specifically he asks himself what we mean by 'useful'. Obviously a plant that cures illness is useful, but isn't a cut flower useful as well? What system of values is it that fails to attribute usefulness to beauty?

The problem is compounded in the article 'The Joys of Angelica'. He says that he personally finds angelica a very beautiful plant to look at, yet he would dismiss any claims that it is efficacious in curing cold stomachs, ulcers, gout, sciatica, lung disease, period pains, wind, and 'plagues and all spirits', as claimed by Culpeper.

I would have been hard pressed to recognise an angelica plant had there not been a line drawing and description in *The Happy Herbalist*. It grows to six or eight feet, has dark green, flattish leaves, a thick but hollow stem, and large heads of white flowers. It grows, I read, in poor conditions and likes damp and semi-shade. It self-seeds readily but the seeds are only viable for a short time.

Ever watchful for symbolism I considered how this description might apply to a woman if there was a person called Angelica who figured in Richard's life. She would be robust, not considered attractive by everybody, shade-loving, (that could mean she didn't share Richard's love of celebrity), fertile, but perhaps only briefly so. And she might or might not be a panacea for the ills that plagued the author. An absolute angel perhaps.

I wasn't sure if this was a far-fetched bit of literary detective work or just a statement of the completely obvious. However, the title article in *A Turn around the Parsley Patch* contains little that is obvious.

The chapter is a disjointed one. Wisden begins by saying that parsley is the king of herbs but that too often it is only used as decoration or in parsley sauce. He suddenly reflects that there is a long tradition of animal imagery used to depict sexuality – the beast with two backs, bitches on heat, beavers, pig parties. These, he properly asserts, demean all concerned, but demean women especially. How much more pleasant, he says, are descriptions of sexuality that use horticultural imagery. He claims that 'the garden' or the 'pleasure garden' is still widely used as a term for the female genitalia, though I can't say they're terms you'll hear bandied about much in the average student bar. He approves of the connotations of health, fertility and order. The labia are the garden gate, the pubic hair is the hedge, and to 'lead someone up the garden path' is to draw them into sexual dalliance.

We discover that angelica is part of the parsley family; then, almost as a punchline, Wisden cites the word parsley as slang for pubic hair. The parsley patch is therefore the female genitalia. After a long day's gardening there's nothing he likes better than a turn around the parsley patch.

I found all this quite entertaining. It wasn't literature, and it wasn't scholarship, but it didn't seem much like standard television fare either. I felt fairly certain that what I had been reading was more enjoyable than most of Gertrude Jekyll.

It was lunchtime. I ate with Stella and asked her to give

47

me her impressions of Richard Wisden. She asked what was all the sudden interest and I said there was no reason. She said she'd found him sexy. I said sexy? She said yes, people you've seen on television are always sexy. I didn't understand that and Stella said she didn't understand it either but it was definitely true. There are many external factors that influence a reading, and the knowledge that your girlfriend met the author and found him sexy is not the least of these. I decided to return to the text.

Wisden writes very well, in an article in his third volume, about the gardens at the Villa Orsini at Bomarzo – an array of fantastic garden features strewn over a steep, rocky site – statues of gods and goddesses, a gateway formed from a giant gargoyle's mouth, an elephant crushing a man, a temple, a ruined amphitheatre. The features are isolated, disconnected, arranged in no logical sequence. Designer and sculptor are unknown but it is supposed that once there was a specified way of walking through the garden that would have provided such a logical sequence, and that there was an allegorical order to be witnessed.

Traditionally the garden is a scene of contemplation and wholeness. A contemplative garden for modern man, says Wisden, must of necessity perplex and disturb, must be fragmentary not whole. The ruins of the Villa Orsini serve him well. He calls it the first modernist garden.

He is seen in a photograph in *The Happy Herbalist* drawing a knot design on the earth, using powdered chalk. He talks about a few famous examples and gives some practical tips on how to make your own. His main advice is to keep it simple. In *Grand Designs* he discusses the knot in more detail and says knots are to be found in carpet designs, in embroidery, bookbinding, wooden panelling and plasterwork.

Wisden quotes George Cavendish who wrote that Wolsey was laying out at Hampton Court 'knottes so enknotted it cannot be exprest'. He also quotes Gervase Markham who says that if a knot design is too elaborate the plan will become too complex for the eye to discern. Wisden asks is the world an unweeded garden, possessed by things rank and gross, or is it a knot of such complexity that it is too 'enknotted' to be expressed or even perceived? If this is hardly a radical train of thought it still seems remarkably heavyweight coming from a television gardening personality.

It was early evening. I had had enough of Richard Wisden for one day. I returned the books to their drawer. Stella was in the kitchen. I told her I wanted to take a turn around the parsley patch. She didn't know what I was talking about. I explained in great detail.

Adults think they're so clever, but they're not as clever as they think they are. If they were really clever they'd know they're not as clever as they think they are.

They also think that I'm stupid, and that isn't very clever of them either. I'm not *very* clever but at least I know it, and in that way I'm cleverer than those adults who aren't clever but think they are.

Look at sex. There's nothing very clever about that, is there? It's just showing off your willy to girls. I don't know what all the fuss is about. I've shown my willy to girls and it's all right but it isn't as good as all that. The girls showed me their slits sometimes and that was sort of interesting but I don't think I could spend my whole life thinking about it and talking about it the way adults do.

None of it would have been so bad if my mother hadn't been trying to educate me herself. All right, she knew more about history, say, than I did but that wasn't surprising when she's been around longer than I have, and it certainly doesn't mean she was clever. I don't know much at all but I'm quite clever with what I do know.

I always knew I should have been at school really but it was all just really stupid. All the teachers hated me. That's why they gave me bad marks. And all the kids hated me and used to say

49

rotten things about me and my mother. I started out being a real baby. I used to cry all the time. Then I started getting my own back and I used to get into fights and I told the teachers they didn't know anything, and I started showing my willy to girls. Everybody still hated me but not as much and not in the same way. Then I got taken away from that school and my mother never bothered to send me to another one.

I used to worry about my mother. She thought I didn't know about her but I did, well I had one or two ideas. She was lazy. Sometimes when she was supposed to be teaching me geography or something she'd just tell me to read a book, a certain bit of it, then she'd say she'd ask me questions about it later. Well she just went to sleep and if I didn't wake her it could be seven or eight in the evening before she came round, and she'd forget to ask me any questions, or she'd even forget what subject we were supposed to be doing.

I blame alcohol. She drank gallons of the stuff. If I drank as much pop as she drank alcohol I'd have been sick all night. Well she wouldn't let me drink that much, and sometimes she *was* sick all night. I think she thought it was clever to drink a lot. I don't. I've drunk quite a lot myself. It's nice at first. I like to mix some gin in with my Tizer. The Tizer doesn't taste much different. It makes you feel giddy. It's all right but I wouldn't want to get addicted like my mother was. We were always short of money because she spent it on drink when she could have spent it on better things like a television.

It was terrible at school, not having a television. They all had computers and videos and we didn't even have a little black and white telly. They used to play games like they were pretending to be characters from the *A Team* or *Miami Vice*. I never knew what they were on about so I couldn't join in, not that they'd have let me join in anyway.

Even if we'd had a television I'd only have wanted to watch the educational programmes and some documentaries, because I think television can be very dangerous in the wrong hands. She said she couldn't afford it. So the only time I ever saw television was when we went to somebody's house and we hardly ever went to anybody's house.

Lots of people came to *our* house, and they brought bottles and loud records and drugs, I think. I'd have to sit in my bedroom and listen to it all through the door and walls, whereas if I'd had a telly it wouldn't have been so bad.

Worst of all my dad was supposed to be rich and he was supposed to be on television all the time. At school they all said I didn't know who my dad was. They all said I hadn't got one. I told them I did and he had his own television programme. They didn't believe me and if they had believed me they'd only have hated me all the more.

I thought my dad was all right. He was a bit old and a bit fat, and he was a bit loud and he never gave us anything, and we didn't see him for years, but when I saw him he was all right. I wish he'd stayed with my mother. I wish he wasn't dead. I thought at first maybe he wasn't dead. My mother could have been lying, but I didn't think she was.

Sometimes I thought the only reason my mother wouldn't let me have a television was because he was on it, but he can't have been on it all that often, can he? I'd have promised not to watch any of his programmes if she'd wanted me to. I can keep promises, not like some adults. Look at marriage. I think they think it's clever to break promises.

All these people came to the house and they used to say, 'See you soon', 'I'll be back again tomorrow', 'I'll have the money for you by the weekend', 'I'll have the stuff for you next week'. They never did. They never came back when they said they were going to come back, and if they came back there was always an argument about why they weren't there yesterday, and they always seemed to be arguing about money. I don't know what the stuff was that they were always discussing. I used to think my mother was a spy and she was selling secrets but I grew out of that idea. I think it must have been drugs but I don't really know what drugs are. People are always going on about drugs but nobody ever explains.

Sometimes these people came on their own and they seemed to come about business. I got sent into the back garden but I saw what went on. Money changed hands, and sometimes my mother seemed to be buying and sometimes she seemed to be selling, and sometimes she had some

51

money and then I got bought some new clothes. Well I'm not interested in new clothes.

Then sometimes there were lots of people who all came together and they had parties and I didn't like that. There was laughing and screaming and loud music and sometimes it went on all night and sometimes I think they had sex. I bet they all thought they were very clever.

If we'd lived somewhere proper like a semi-detached house there'd have been neighbours and they'd have complained and called the police and they'd all have got sent to prison. Some people might think that was a bit harsh but it would have served them right. There might have been a shoot-out and someone might have got killed but that would have been just too bad.

I never really knew what my mother was doing but I didn't like it and I always hoped she'd get caught for her own good. I thought they must know about her, surely, the police or somebody. I always wanted them to come and put a stop to it, so when Johnny Fantham arrived, well, it was the answer to all my prayers.

We took David to the hospital in my car. We said little on the journey but it was impossible to tell whether Angelica's silence was caused by shock, by the anaesthetising effects of marijuana, or by indifference. I was much occupied by trying to construct an even moderately convincing account of events that would satisfy the hospital without requiring any serious police involvement.

I told David to say he had found the gun in an unlocked kitchen cupboard, and loaded it himself despite his mother's dire warnings never to do such a thing. Then while attempting to shoot a rabbit, he had accidentally shot himself in the calf. The story had the inauthentic ring of truth, and it made Angelica appear careless rather than homicidal. A policeman, rural and avuncular, might call to give Angelica a stern lecture on the proper storage of shotguns, but I hoped that would be all. David seemed more than happy to play along with the pretence.

The hospital was better than I had any right to expect. There was northern warmth, tea dispensed as a universal panacea; and a shotgun wound was obviously a novelty for them. I spoke with a young, fair, prematurely balding doctor whom I outranked and who agreed that David should be kept for a few nights to give the desolate mother some respite. David was extremely brave in a comic sort of way, and at seven that evening we left him for the night.

I tried to get Angelica to talk about Richard. It was hard work. We were sitting in a pub in Chesterfield where the landlord did not seem to approve of two women drinking alone together.

I said to Angelica, 'I don't understand why you wanted to shoot at the detective.'

She said, 'Because I've had enough of people snooping around here. Some of them were the law. Some were worse.'

'You're extremely lucky it wasn't the "law".'

'I'm past caring.'

I said, 'Do you know who the man was?' She didn't and I explained. 'I was wondering,' I said, 'how he came to have a key to the boot of your car.'

'It isn't my car. One of Richard's floozies dumped it here.'

'What was in the boot?'

'How should I know? I didn't have a key, did I?'

'But this man did.'

'So?'

'I find that interesting. I'm surprised you don't. And wouldn't you like to know what was in that boot?'

'Why should I?'

'It might reveal something about Richard's death.'

Angelica said, 'He's dead, isn't he? What good is revealing anything going to do? What does it matter?'

I said, 'What if Richard was murdered? Would that matter?'

'Not to Richard.'

'But surely it would make some difference to those of us left behind.'

She finished her drink and indicated that I should buy her another one. I did not want to be too drunk to drive back to London, but the flow of drink was making Angelica considerably more forthcoming.

She said, 'I was in love with him, whatever that means. I didn't know what to do about it. I should have let him build me a knot garden. He might still be alive.'

I said, 'Did he love you?'

'Doesn't look like it, does it? If he really loved me he wouldn't have killed himself.'

'*If* he killed himself.'

Angelica did not seem able to entertain this possibility. She said, 'He was only in love with one person.'

I recalled his arrogance, his confidence, his smugness, and I said, 'You mean himself.'

'I mean Libby.'

I said, 'But surely their marriage was nothing more than a convenient legal contract. They led completely separate lives.'

'Yes, but that was never his idea, it was hers. I don't know if she was ever in love with him, but let's give her the benefit of the doubt and say that she was when they first married. But it wore off.

'I can't blame her. He was a bastard to live with. In the early days of their marriage he was still chasing anything in skirts, and she probably didn't see that much of him. He was working, so was she. They didn't have any children. They didn't have any friends or interests in common. It wouldn't have been hard to fall out of love.

'The only problem was, Richard didn't fall out of love. He was still madly in love with that bitch. He didn't want to settle for this polite, civilised deal where they carried on living under the same roof, enjoying the tax advantages and not feeling anything for each other.'

I said, 'Angelica, that was precisely the "deal" he did settle for.'

'Because that was the only deal Libby was offering. He loved her and that was the most he could get from her. He thought that if he hung around long enough then she'd change her mind. He thought she'd fall in love with him again.

'I told him he was crazy. I told him over and over again that there was no way she was ever going to want him like he wanted her. For a long time he didn't believe me. He was sure she'd come round. Then one day I think he did believe me, and that's when he committed suicide.

'If you're looking for a murderer, even if you're only looking for somebody to dump the blame on, you've got two really good suspects. One of them's her, for making his life a misery. The other one's me for making him see just how miserable his life was.'

I have little personal experience with suicide cases, yet common sense tells me that it is absurd to burden anyone else with the responsibility for one's own suicide. We are responsible for ourselves. We have some duty to others, and a right to expect some consideration from them, but if that expectation is disappointed, if that consideration is not forthcoming, I don't believe it can ever be true to say that someone killed themselves 'because of' another person.

If Richard did commit suicide, nobody was responsible for his death but him. And yet, when I thought of Libby Wisden it seemed that Angelica's account made good sense. Richard, for all I disliked him, appeared to have every reason to live. Yet, if the one person he loved considered him to be worthless, and if that one person were someone as desirable and complete as Libby, then those reasons for living might seem very empty indeed.

Richard was not Libby's equal. How then could he expect to be loved by as rare a woman as she? If he had realised how hopeless and worthless, how petty his life truly was, then who could blame him for ending it? Perhaps he would have been perfectly content if he had chosen some attractive but ordinary girl who would have shared his success without making too many demands, someone like Angelica. Yes, his tragedy, if he could be said to be tragic, was that he had aimed too high.

Angelica had become sullen and mute. I felt I would get no more out of her. We sat silently for some time. Two men tried to sit down at our table and 'chat us up'. I hardly felt that Angelica and I, tired and aging, were the best catches to be had in Chesterfield that night. Angelica told them to 'piss off' before they even sat down. The two men did not argue but left immediately, muttering darkly as they went that we were a 'pair of lesbians'. I have been called worse.

I mean to say, I'm not anybody's idea of a hero. I'm not a coward but I'm not exactly SAS material either. They'd got my kid. I mean I'd kill anybody who laid a finger on Diane but who were these blokes? Who was Vesta Security? How was I ever going to get at them? What the hell did any of it have to do with me, anyway? I wasn't going to risk my daughter for the sake of some dead bloke, for some used tenners, for the sake of some insurance claim. I did what they told me to do. I didn't feel proud of myself, but I did it.

I phoned Libby Wisden and said I wanted to see her. She invited me round. The place was unbelievable – Hampstead, swimming pool, big garden, high walls. She showed me into the front room. It was hot and maybe that was why she still hadn't got many clothes on.

'Tell me what you've discovered,' she said.

'Not much,' I said. 'Really, not much.'

'Meaning?'

'I mean, I don't think there was all that much to discover.'

'No?'

'No. Your husband killed himself.'

'You think so.'

'I know so. He booked into the hotel, took a lot of drink and sleeping pills. Curtains.'

'And the girl?'

'Girl?'

'Don't be difficult, Mr Fantham. The girl in the photographs.'

56

'Just some girl,' I said. 'Just some girl he picked up. He decided to go out with a bang.'

'You said you knew her. You even told me her name.'

'I was wrong there. I did think it was someone I knew but I was wrong. I mean they're not very clear photographs. There are a lot of little blonde tarts around, aren't there?'

I could see that Libby Wisden wasn't buying very much of this and I couldn't really blame her. I mean I never claimed to be a super sleuth but nobody could be quite as bad as I was pretending to be.

'What about the other photographs?' she asked. 'The ones taken in the gardens.'

'No idea,' I said. 'I spent a whole day in the library going through reference books with pictures of gardens. Didn't come up with a sausage.'

'And what of the contents of Richard's suitcase? Didn't they mean something?'

'Why does everything have to mean something?' I said. 'They're just what he happened to have in his suitcase at the time.'

'Is something wrong, Mr Fantham?'

'Eh?'

'Is someone putting pressure on you? Has somebody offered you more money than I did? Who?'

'Calm down, blossom,' I said. 'Nobody's got to me. Nobody's offered me more money, but you can have all your bloody money back if you don't think you've had what you paid for.'

'The money means more to you than it does to me,' she said. 'But you've confused me, Mr Fantham. You seem not to have discovered anything about Richard's death, yet you began by saying you were sure he committed suicide.'

'Yes,' I said. 'I found this.'

I gave her a white envelope. It had her name on it, written in a fair forgery of Richard Wisden's handwriting.

'What's this?' she said.

'I don't know. It looks like it might be a suicide note. That's just a guess.'

'Where did you find it?'

57

'In the hotel room, under the carpet. I don't know how the police missed it.'

She opened the envelope and looked at the letter inside. I knew what it was going to say. I should have done. After all, I'd written it.

It said:

Dear Libby,
This is the end. I have decided to kill myself. I've had enough. I have moved into the Hancock to do it without fuss and bother. There are no suspicious circumstances, honestly.
Love,
Richard

I'd typed it out on a machine in the hotel. I thought that was a nice touch. Besides I didn't think I could have kept up the forgery for a whole letter, even a short one. Libby Wisden read it and laughed.

'I think you're quite sweet, Mr Fantham,' she said. 'But either you're very dim or you think I am.'

'Pardon?'

'Either that or you're very frightened.'

I couldn't see any point in trying to brazen it out with her.

'I'm scared shitless,' I said. 'They've threatened to hurt my daughter.'

'Who has?'

'I don't know. I mean, I really don't know but I wouldn't tell even if I did. They mean business whoever they are. I've done what they told me. I came here and told you I hadn't found out anything about your husband's death, that it all pointed to suicide.'

'But it seems to me, Mr Fantham, that everything you've told me points rather to the reverse. You've told me a lot, albeit obliquely. Is there no way I can make you tell me more?'

'Money doesn't interest me quite as much as you seem to think it does.'

'I wasn't only thinking about money.'

I was on my feet and out of that place in two seconds flat.

I mean I've been offered pussy in some funny places and at some funny times but that really took the prize. What did she take me for? Did she really think I was going to risk my daughter for a bit of the other? Do me a favour.

I went back to my flat, back where I belonged, a run-down conversion in Notting Hill. The place was empty – no family, no gorillas, nothing.

The next day I opened a building society account in Diane's name. I put in all the money I'd got from Libby Wisden which I hadn't touched a penny of. I went back to the Hancock. There'd been a fight in the Stable bar. Two daft bastards had been fighting over some bird. Why would anybody want to do a thing like that? They'd have to be out of their minds.

If Richard Wisden's essence was to be found in his written work, and I was by no means certain that it was, then it seemed to me to be found most intensely in two essays in *A Turn around the Parsley Patch*. The first is the dirty weekend piece called 'On the Balcony'. The second is 'A Contemplative Garden for 20th Century Man'.

In 'On the Balcony' the author and his unnamed mistress visit the Lake District and stay in a small hotel famous for the quality of its food. That, however, is not the only reason for their being there. Richard Wisden writes:

We were there to fuck, to hump, to shag, to have rumpy-pumpy, jig-a-jig, to do it, to make love, to pleasure, to know each other in the biblical sense, to dick, fornicate, bang, go the whole way, to score, to screw, to skin the cat, to roger, to rifle, to rasp and rattle and rabbit and rut, and to indulge in a thousand and one other euphemisms for doing what comes naturally.

And that's not all. His mistress, he tells us, is highly adept at oral sex or, as he puts it, 'gobbling, gnawing the 'nana, and eating breakfast in bed'. In the course of the weekend he finds her 'ripe and juicy', he enjoys 'the vinegar stroke', he has an excess of 'crumpet', of the old 'bacon sandwich' or 'chopped liver'. He enjoys a 'boxed lunch'. His mistress sings the praises of his 'vegetable stick'. Wisden establishes, rather exhaustingly, an undeniable connection between food, sex and language.

Then we hear what was, in the literal sense, eaten over the weekend. There is leek terrine with feta and walnuts, artichoke hearts with dandelion and cream, oysters in Guinness batter, and avocado stuffed with smoked chicken soufflé. Main courses include fillet steak with blackberry and shallot sauce, roast mallard, lemon sole and red mullet combined in a beurre blanc and served in puff pastry with a spinach and nutmeg sauce. The sweets, I'm glad to say, defy description. Then comes the drink – La Côte aux Enfants, Ay Rouge, Chassagne Montrachet, pernod frappé, peppermint schnapps.

It doesn't stop at the bedroom door either. In the bed Wisden drinks Benedictine from the mistress's navel, then sparkling English gooseberry wine from her vagina. They pass hazelnut and guava sorbet from mouth to mouth, and he bedecks her nipples with slivers of smoked pigeon breast.

On the final day of the holiday Wisden develops, to his surprise, though scarcely to ours, nausea and brewer's droop, and despite, in his own words, much 'jerkin' of the gherkin' he remains limp. The mistress is extremely supportive but he is inconsolable. Wisden lies slumped in a chair on the hotel's balcony. His mistress brings him a plate of Turkish delight and he seems to think this is all deeply symbolic of something or other though he can't actually articulate what. Nor for that matter can I. What exactly is symbolised by a fat man on a balcony, overfed, hungover, and unable to get an erection? Is this perhaps twentieth-century Western man? I think Wisden thinks so.

And so we come to the article 'A Contemplative Garden for 20th Century Man'. It is short for such a crucial text but Wisden has strewn fairly broad hints about what he has in mind here; the symbolic garden that fails to symbolise, a ruined site, an unweeded plot that is possessed by things rank and gross, a knot which cannot be untied.

A weed he says, agreeing I think with Vita Sackville-West, is a plant in the wrong place, a plant that does not fit into our plan for the garden, into our scheme of how things ought to be arranged. Wisden describes the back-breaking toil of weeding. He wonders as he weeds whether *he* is in the wrong place. He wonders what will be left of his works once he is dead, when he's 'pushing up the daisies'. How long does it take for the cultivated plants to be choked out? How long before his design becomes smudged and unintelligible? As he works he sees that he is fighting a losing battle. He is fighting against nature, a nature that despises neat flowerbeds, trim lawns and polite little rose bushes, and he knows he is destined to lose.

As he sets out his knots, his formal arrangements of complementary colour and shape, he knows that the ground has other 'capabilities' to which it will return – a return to wildness, disorder and death.

Wisden sees himself old, impotent, bereft of strength or ideas, an old man on a sun-lounger, a strong drink in his hand, the evening turning cold and the weeds taking over. He lies in the dark, waiting for death. 'The horror. The horror.' 'Mistah Wisden – he dead.'

What was one to make of it? Is this irony? Is it a joke? One asks to what extent Wisden is being serious, and I am forced to conclude that he is, alas, being perfectly serious. He claims to have looked, in however local and quotidian a way, into some personal heart of darkness.

And having done so, what should he do next? Become a god? Kill himself? Perhaps the article 'A Contemplative Garden for 20th Century Man' is, in fact, an elaborate suicide note.

I think most people meeting me for the first time, indeed after many times, would say I was a rather dull character. 'Basil Shaw,' they'd say, 'nice enough chap, moderately successful, quite good at his job in the bank, dull as ditchwater.' I wouldn't argue because I have no need to. I have seen and done things that most men in the street only dream. I am talking about sex – wild orgies, hot and hasty couplings, fevered acts of passion, Dionysian sensuality, dirty fucking (pardon my French). The fact is, I am a 'slave' to pleasure.

However, I think you will concede, this kind of pleasure is not come by easily or accidentally. These things don't just 'happen'. Or, to put it another way, it takes a lot of hard work and a certain amount of organisational flair to make them happen.

Hence the Posthumous Society. It is defunct now of course. It was disbanded a few years ago, but it feels like a lifetime, and in today's climate it seems like an institution from a different age entirely.

I was one of the society's guiding lights. I was on the committee. I was in charge of organising discussion groups, and I was membership secretary and archivist, with all that that entails. It took up exorbitant amounts of time but I knew no better way of spending that time.

The post of membership secretary was particularly time consuming. One had to keep careful track of members, of changes of address, to keep the records straight and the standards up, to retain the balance between male and female, age and youth, technical prowess and raw enthusiasm. Potential members weren't vetted exactly, that makes us sound like MI5, but we liked to see photographs of them, read their application forms, and if possible we liked to discuss their membership with existing members who knew the applicant. If we had doubts we conducted a personal interview and if any doubts remained we preferred to be safe than sorry.

My role was obviously a delicate one. Our members were a genuine mix, but they tended to be of professional status with high disposable incomes. We had about three hundred members and they included architects, bankers, university lecturers, musicians, and several moderately famous broadcasters and television personalities. These were people with a lot to lose. It was just as well that my integrity was beyond question, and of course, as a big wheel at the bank I had as much to lose as anyone.

We considered two ways to ensure absolute discretion. First we thought of operating in conditions of total anonymity – no names, no photographs, no personal details. Members might have been given numbers or fictitious names, and that would have been all that was known of them.

This was rejected precisely because one or two members were already public figures and the adoption of a false name would not have given these people the same protection it afforded to those outside the public gaze. The no-photographs rule would also have displeased the many people who listed the taking of photographs as one of their particular pleasures.

So we opted for the very opposite. The membership files give exhaustive details of names, addresses, sexual inclinations, personal histories, full-face photograph, and the all-important 'initiation portrait'.

Let me explain the initiation portrait. The application form that potential members had to fill in had one apparently insignificant section on page 6. After giving details of all the many things you had done, would like to do, or would like to watch being done etc. etc., there was a small heading that said 'List here those activities you do not wish to perform'. This produced a colourful selection of highly imaginative taboos.

If we decided we wanted the new applicant to be one of 'us' we requested that he or she perform at least one of the acts they had named in this section, and be photographed performing it. The photograph went into the files and stayed there in 'perpetuity'. We felt this was an excellent way to guarantee discretion. This way each of us was equally compromised and we ruled out the chance of blackmail while ensuring a certain solidarity both at the time and in the future.

Some people found the performance of this undesired act impossible. Here we were often happy to compromise but in most cases the single performance of this act was seen as a rite of passage and a small price to pay for admission to a world of sexual ecstasy.

Please don't think we wished to make members do anything they didn't want to do. However it was sometimes surprising what people wished to do once they realised that almost anything was permitted. We called nothing 'unnatural' and it could be most surprising to discover what people had in their natures.

Look at Richard Wisden. When he joined the society he wanted lots and lots of straightforward intercourse with lots of different women. I believe he described it as 'variety'. I think we made him understand that this was a very limited definition of variety. Richard described his dislikes as 'pain of all sorts, bondage, homosexual activity, fetishism, transvestism et al'. His initiation portrait shows him bound, dressed in fishnet stockings, his penis being fondled by an elderly gent, while one of our ladies offers a cane to his bare buttocks.

Unlike some similar organisations the Posthumous Society did not rule out the membership of single males, and it was as a single male that Richard Wisden joined us. We all thought that was a terrible shame since we knew he had an exquisitely beautiful wife. I had always hoped that she might join us.

You can imagine my surprise, some years after the demise of the Posthumous Society, to find Libby Wisden appearing in my office at the bank. Her husband had hardly been dead a week and I expressed my very real sadness. I assumed she had come for advice on death duties and the management of trusts. I was taken aback when she explained she was there because she was interested in the Posthumous Society.

'What do you mean by "interested"?' I said.

'I think I'd like to join.'

You understand it was years since I'd had such a request,

and I doubt if I had ever had a request from such a 'worthy' applicant as Libby Wisden. You can imagine the regret with which I told her that the Posthumous Society was no more.

'But surely,' she said, 'once a member, always a member.'

'I'm sorry?'

'You must still know who the members were. You must still have names and addresses and phone numbers. I assume you must still have your membership files.'

'Of course,' I said, although I wondered how she knew I was still in possession of the files, or that there had ever been such files.

'Then you could ring a few people. I'm sure you could arrange some sort of ad hoc meeting.'

'It won't be easy,' I said, warming to the idea even as I contemplated the difficulties. 'People move house. They become settled and staid. They have families. They get worried about disease. And who can really blame them?'

'I can blame them,' she said. 'But surely a few of them would come out of hiding if there was sufficient attraction. I could be such an attraction.'

She was absolutely correct. The more I thought about it the more I felt sure that Libby Wisden would be enough of a pull to bring half a dozen or so of the former members out of hibernation. I said I would do my best to organise a 'reunion' at which Libby would be guest of honour. She said that sounded 'ideal'.

'There's one thing I must ask,' I said. 'Why is it that you wanted to join the Posthumous Society after your husband's death, yet you chose not to when he was alive?'

'Perhaps,' she said, 'you think I'm trying to bury my feelings of guilt in a savage bout of loveless promiscuity.'

'Perhaps I do.'

'The reason I didn't want to join while my husband was alive is that I seldom wanted to be in the same room as my husband, certainly not while there was any sexual activity going on.'

That failed to convince me and she must have seen scepticism in my face for she then continued, 'But in a way you're right to suspect an ulterior motive. I came to see you because

I want to know why and how Richard died, and I think you can tell me.'

'Me?'

She nodded.

'I'm flattered that you think I knew your husband that well, but really I didn't. I'm afraid I don't see how I can be of any service.'

'What if we went through your old Posthumous Society files? I'm sure we could find something.'

'We might find all sorts of things. What particular sort of thing did you have in mind?'

'I shan't know that until I've looked.'

'But my files are strictly confidential.'

'Or perhaps you don't want me to be guest of honour at your little reunion.'

No doubt I should have seen this coming but I did not. Was this a threat? Blackmail? If the latter it was the sweetest and most persuasive form of blackmail I could have imagined. While the archives are confidential they hardly contain state secrets, and they do not contain information that is unobtainable elsewhere. The details of dates of birth, addresses, careers, were given out freely at meetings in the old days. And even though the files contained information about sexual preferences and idiosyncrasies, again these preferences and idiosyncrasies were very frequently revealed, not to say 'paraded' at some of the meetings. I was therefore unlikely to be spilling any madly confidential 'beans', and I would also be helping to console the widow of one of our most valued 'former' members.

'Very well,' I said, 'after the reunion we can spend an evening together going through the archives, though I'm by no means certain you'll find what you're looking for.'

'Then thank you for indulging me, anyway,' she said, and she smiled a very disarming smile.

'I understand,' she continued, 'that you used to hold little initiations for new members.'

I wasn't best pleased that such an intimate part of our procedures had 'leaked out', but it was as pointless to be angry as it was to deny it. Instead I asked her how she would

66

have filled in that part of our application form that asks what activities she would not wish to perform.

'I'd have left it blank,' she said. 'I like it all. There's nothing I won't do.'

I decided I would have to come up with something a little special for Mrs Libby Wisden.

My dad always wanted me to call him Richard. I just wanted to call him Dad, but he didn't like that. I don't know why. So I didn't call him anything really. He used to bring me presents. They weren't much when you consider how rich he was supposed to be, but I know it's the thought that counts. I wish my mother would remember that more often. He'd bring me books. I can't read all that well but the books had lots of pictures in them and that was a help, but they were always pictures of flowers and things and I didn't like that very much.

He always wanted to go for walks so I'd go out with him. I think he was trying to get away from my mother. He'd make me take a book and I'd have to spot flowers and things. I wasn't any good at it. It was like being at school. I didn't care if I was no good at school, but I wanted to be good at this because it was my dad. He was better than school because he didn't get mad like they did.

He used to say it didn't matter if you couldn't put a name to things so long as you enjoyed the things themselves. He said there was nothing clever about it. I was glad, but I don't like flowers much. They all looked the same and I thought it was a bit wet.

What was worse than having to spot things was that he used to try to make me eat things, dandelions and wild mushrooms and things. I thought they must be all covered in germs. When he came and stayed at the house he'd always do the cooking. He thought he was really good but I didn't. Everything always had bits of plant in it. He called them herbs and he said things always tasted better with herbs, but I didn't think so.

The only thing I did like was some stuff called angelica. I didn't understand why it had the same name as my mother. I thought it was a joke at first but they both said it was true so I suppose I believe them, though I know you can't trust adults. Angelica was all sweet tasting and I liked it. It wasn't straight from the garden. They did things to it first.

I thought it was funny my mother having the same name as a plant. I thought it might be important. My dad said there were lots of people with the same names as plants. I remember we were having a walk and he listed loads of them. Most of them I'd never heard of. I hadn't heard of the plants and I hadn't heard of people having those names. I know about names like Rose but my dad's ones were really weird.

I used to think my dad was a clever man, properly clever, not just thinking he was, like the others. He used to say he wasn't, but if he was rich and if he was on television and he knew all about these plants, well he must have been fairly clever, I think. He must have been cleverer than my mother because he had a new car and he went to interesting places. He told me that cars didn't mean anything, and having money and being on television didn't mean anything, but I didn't believe him. I don't think he was lying to me. I think he was just wrong.

What was the best thing about him coming to stay was that it made all the other people keep away. Him and my mother would stay up all night talking and they'd both drink quite a lot and they'd put music on but not too loud because my dad cared about not keeping me awake. It was all really a lot better when he came.

I don't know why the people didn't come. They might have been scared of him but he wasn't really scarey. I think my mother must have told them not to come because she didn't want my dad to know what she got up to when he wasn't there because he wouldn't have liked it and he'd have used

68

his influence to get it all sorted out and make her stop. My dad had a lot of influence.

I don't know if they really liked each other. He seemed to like her more than she liked him but you can never tell with adults. They used to kiss a lot but they used to argue a lot as well so I don't know.

I didn't know my dad all that long. He started coming to see us about two years ago, I think. I don't know where he'd been. I don't know why he couldn't come and see us before that. He said he'd seen me when I was a baby, but I don't know if he really had.

He was always talking about doing things with the garden. I thought it sounded a good idea. I thought if he did it really well we could charge people to come and look at it, then we'd be well off. My mother told me not to be silly, but I didn't think it was at all silly. Lots of people pay money to go and look at gardens. I don't know why, but they do.

In fact I think she was silly because if she'd had the garden done it would have been something to remember him by now that he was dead. I told my mother this and she said she didn't need anything to remind her of him because she'd got me. I didn't really understand that.

My dad brought me other things besides books. There were footballs and tennis balls but they always got lost in the garden. He used to call it the jungle. He made some paper aeroplanes and we had this game. I'd be upstairs in my bedroom and I'd open the window and set one of the paper planes on fire and I'd throw it out of the window into the garden and it was like a plane crash in the jungle. I'd pretend to be the rescue party and my dad would pretend to be a survivor from the plane and I'd have to rescue him. He was good at it because he'd be lots of different people and he could do different voices, and sometimes he'd pretend to be really badly injured and I'd have to try to drag him out of the jungle and sometimes he'd be so badly injured that he'd die out there in the jungle and I'd pretend to be the priest and say a few words over the corpse. It was great.

He also bought me a water-pistol. It was pink and it was like a ray-gun. I'd use it to put out the fire in the paper planes.

69

Usually the fire went out by the time it hit the garden but one time my dad had filled up the water-pistol with that stuff you put in cigarette lighters and the plane was still on fire and I squirted that stuff on out of the water-pistol and it was like an explosion. There weren't any survivors that time.

Then there was the time with the bleach. My dad wasn't there so there was a party going on and it was winter and everybody had thrown their coats on my mother's bed and they all thought I was asleep but I wasn't. So I loaded up the water-pistol with bleach and I sprayed it all over the coats. I got hit for that but it was worth it.

So when this man called Johnny Fantham arrived I knew he was on my side because he'd got the water-pistol and obviously that was some sort of secret sign. Plus he had the key to the boot of the car and I'd known all along there was something fishy about that car.

I didn't like the look of the girl who brought it, and I didn't like the look of the woman who came and said she was a doctor. I didn't like the look of her and I thought she was up to no good.

Even without the water-pistol I'd have known that Johnny Fantham was a good guy. It was obvious, but I was still careful. I didn't want to give anything away so I played dumb. I wanted to know what was in that boot as much as he did. I thought it might be a body.

I knew my mother had a shotgun. She said it was to shoot rabbits but I knew better. I couldn't let her get away with it. I had to cause a diversion. I did and it worked very well. Johnny got what he came for. I got hurt in the leg but that was a small price to pay.

It turned out the woman probably was a real doctor. She knew what to do with my leg. I got taken to hospital. It was great. Everybody said I was being very brave. They treated me a bit like a child but I didn't hold it against them.

It didn't hurt nearly as much as I thought it would. I had to stay in hospital for quite a while. I didn't mind at all. My mother went off with the doctor woman. I didn't like that. I wondered if she was in any danger. It was just as well she'd got the shotgun and wasn't afraid to use it.

The nurses were great. They do a marvellous job. Next day they offered me books and comics but I was only interested in television. I said I didn't have one at home and I got lots of sympathy. They wouldn't let me get out of bed but they turned the set round so I could see it. It was a big set. The colour wasn't very good but I couldn't complain. A few days passed.

Then I had my first visitor. I knew something was up. I knew I must have stumbled into something really big. She was nice looking on the surface, really beautiful, but I knew I couldn't trust her. She looked like a model or something. She sat down on the chair next to the bed and said,

'Hello David. You don't know me but my name's Libby Wisden.'

Michel Foucault and I are as near as damn it in agreement on the problems of what constitutes a 'work' and what constitutes an 'author'. Richard Wisden did not define himself as an author. He was a gardener, a designer, a television performer, who in the course of his work, happened to write. His 'works' therefore are not delineated by the boundaries of his books. They include the gardens he made, the plans he drew, the instructions he set down for subcontractors, the programmes he made for television.

If I were employed to locate Richard Wisden in the largest sense I would have been out and about visiting the gardens of his clients, reading his letters, his accounts, examining notes and drawings, watching recordings on video tape. I was extremely thankful that my brief did not extend to locating the whole man.

I made an appointment to see Libby Wisden and then I made the quite devastating mistake of telling Stella about the

71

work I had been doing on Richard Wisden's books. The consequences of this you will see.

Next day I caught the train to London, took a tube to the Wisden house in Hampstead. The house was compact and no doubt hysterically expensive, being a geometric arrangement of glass and red brick, softened by lots of greenery.

We met in the galleried lounge. The furniture was hard and squeaky. The walls were full of modern prints that I imagine could be bought by the square yard to match the existing decor. I was feeling more than a little cynical about the affairs of Mr and Mrs Wisden.

I told her I thought that Richard wrote moderately well. He was quirky, entertaining, readable. She smiled through all this as though I was complimenting her on owning a well-behaved dog. But I said I felt words like 'quirky', 'entertaining', 'readable', were assessments that might satisfy a blurb writer, yet would not do for a literary critic, not that I had ever previously described myself as a literary critic exactly.

I said I found the writings of Richard Wisden essentially hollow. The descriptions of herbs, of meals eaten, of dirty weekends enjoyed, failed to convey any feeling of truth. This was not to say that the descriptions were not factually accurate, nor the emotions deeply felt; however, by the time any language reached the page it had made whatever experience it dealt with seem utterly bogus.

I said I was crucially unconvinced by Wisden's claimed insights into despair, chaos, nature and death. These were merely petty literary conceits. They were adolescent posturings and as such might be forgiven in an adolescent, but were to be despised in a grown man.

Libby Wisden's elegant little face became strangely uncomposed. She was perturbed by the strength of my feelings. Was I not reading more into the text than was actually there? Wasn't I, at the very least, over-reacting? I told her I didn't think so. She said it seemed that I was letting personal feelings cloud my judgment. I said there was a world out there, a real world where people really lived and died, had real feelings of love and hate, experienced genuine pain and loss; and the author of *The Happy Herbalist*, *Grand Designs*, and *A Turn around the Parsley Patch* had no access to that world or to those feelings, much as he wanted to have, and much as he might pile on the fine words to convince the reader that he did. I said also that I thought rich widows might find better things to do with their money than employ academics who would inevitably loathe them and all that they stood for.

She took it all very well. I wondered if we were going to have a literary debate but we had a drink instead. She was not a stupid woman and she asked me to tell her what the *real* problem was, and like a fool I found myself telling her.

I told her about the conversation I had had with Stella the previous day. I had told Stella about my visit from Libby Wisden, about the books and the money. Stella in her turn had told me that the chance meeting she had had with Richard Wisden was not at all as she had previously described. The meeting had indeed taken place in a pub in Lambeth at lunchtime, and Stella had certainly told him that she admired his work and he had shyly accepted the praise. However, he was not too shy to invite Stella to accompany him on a visit to the Tradescant Garden in the redundant church of St Mary at Lambeth. There, amid the interlocking circles of box with the letter T spelled out three times in grey *Santolina incana* beside the tomb of Captain Bligh, Richard Wisden was not too shy to ask Stella to accompany him to a hotel for the afternoon. And Stella had agreed. This had not been, as I had at first hoped and imagined, an event that had taken place years ago before I knew and loved and lived with Stella, but rather something that had happened in all too recent times.

I told Libby Wisden I was not sure what kind of game was being played, and I did not understand why I'd been selected as a participant. I did not know what she wanted from me, and I did not particularly want to find out.

She told me she had not known about Richard and Stella, that it was all coincidence, that there was nothing to worry about, that no game was being played, that I was not being used. I was almost tempted to believe her, yet it made no difference whether I believed her or not.

I left her house and went to a pub. I stayed there till closing time. I got to Liverpool Street in time to catch the last train

73

home. When the train arrived at my own station there were no more taxis and I reluctantly had to ring Stella and ask her to come and drive me home. I was careful not to ask her to 'pick me up'.

We drove the few miles home. I was sober. I said I'd been in the wrong and she did not contradict me. I said I couldn't really explain why I felt so hurt and angry. She told me, as she had told me before, that the event hadn't meant anything to her, and she seemed to think I ought to feel better for this. I told her that events may have meanings quite other than the ones we personally assign to them.

The night was cold and Stella had lit a small fire in the living room. I felt a certain Nazi thrill, also a certain Liberal horror, as I threw the complete works of Richard Wisden into the flames. It seemed the natural thing to do with them.

The room was set for Libby Wisden's arrival, for her first encounter with the Posthumous Society, for her initiation. The meetings used to take place in my own Victorian town-house in Clapham, and this new one was no exception. I had made extensive preparations. The room was dark. The central heating was on. There was soft music issuing from the stereo.

She was slightly late but one had no reason to complain. She was a vision. She was wearing a black silk dress that stirred the imagination. It was short and backless and she wore nothing beneath. Its smooth contours caressed her buttocks and gave unmistakeable hints about her firm, full breasts. Her legs were long and lean and bare. Her make-up was heavy but expertly applied. I gave her a soft kiss of welcome and detected the strong tang of alcohol on her breath.

'I needed a little Dutch courage,' she said.

'I thought you had no shortage of courage,' I bantered.

She smiled a little nervously and looked about the room.

'I assumed there'd be others,' she said.

'There will be,' I said. 'Now please take your clothes off.'

In one movement she had rid herself of the dress. She stood naked before me. It was a pretty sight. Her body was fresh and firm and bronzed all over. I felt some stirrings in my loins, or perhaps in my head. I picked up her dress, folding it carefully, thrilling at the way it retained heat from Libby's body.

'Sit down,' I said. 'Be comfortable.'

She selected an armchair decorated in peacock fabric and sank into its contours. I reached into a drawer in the sideboard and removed a small walnut box. I opened it and showed it to Libby. The box contained a child's water-pistol, but there was nothing childlike about the uses to which I was about to put it.

I clapped my hands and six members of the Posthumous Society came in from the dining room where they had been secreted. There were three men and three women, representing a pleasing cross-section of ages, body shapes and sexual preferences.

'Modesty' forbids me describing the exact rituals that constituted Libby's initiation; modesty and a belief that a secret society has to have *some* secrets. Suffice it to say that certain intimate acts took place involving male and female genitalia, several types of bodily fluid, and, of course, a water-pistol; acts undreamed of by the toy manufacturer.

I must say that Libby threw herself into the activities with determination if not with observable delight. I took a back seat while the initiation was going on, my participation limited to snapping with my Polaroid. Once the ceremony was completed I handed round my efforts and assured Libby that she was now truly one of 'us'.

I made introductions between Libby and the others whom she had known only 'carnally' until now. She seemed polite but reserved.

I opened a couple of bottles, changed the music to Ella

Fitzgerald and it was my sincere hope that an informal orgy would now take place. It did not. This can sometimes happen after an initiation. The intensity of that event can be so great that further activity seems pale by comparison.

Libby was particularly disappointing. She remained in a chair claiming she was 'worn out'. I felt a little glum. Certainly Libby had performed her initiatory task, but I felt she had obeyed the letter rather than the spirit of the thing. She had seemed eager enough to participate but I wondered now if she had only been eager to get it over with. She then drank rather a lot, rather quickly, and made neither physical nor verbal contact with anyone. At 11.15 she 'made her excuses' and left, saying she was late for dinner with a 'friend'.

I saw her out to a cab, handed her half the Polaroids I had taken, and gave her a chaste kiss on the cheek.

'First meetings can often be a little strained,' I said.

'I'm sure there'll be others,' she said.

'I hope so.'

'When I can look through the files.'

'Of course,' I said. 'Did you think I might not keep my bargain?'

'I didn't know,' she said. 'Let's make it very soon.'

I agreed. When I returned to the room there was a far more relaxed atmosphere prevailing. Someone asked me where I'd found the 'ice maiden' and I had to say she had found me. Before long there was gentle coupling taking place in various parts of the room. Ella Fitzgerald was singing 'Every Time We Say Goodbye'. I reached for my Polaroid.

I drove from Derbyshire to London. Both night and motorway were clear, though my head was a little thick with drink and tiredness. I kept the car windows open to stay awake. I had pressed some money into Angelica's hand and deposited her outside a decent-looking bed and breakfast establishment.

I returned to London. I returned to my work. In the following days I attempted to speak to Libby but failed. I left messages on her answering machine that told the story of the Derbyshire episode in as much detail as that mode of communication would allow. I had no way of knowing whether she received those messages but certainly she did not return my calls.

My surgeries were as banal as ever. The patient arrives demanding 'health'. He knows health is a thing worth possessing and he believes I am in business to supply it. He wishes to obtain health from me as he might obtain money from a bank or a new three-piece suite from a furniture shop.

If the body is a symbol of anything it is a symbol of time and death. I see the skull beneath the skin but frankly I do not find that so very disagreeable. Bone is hard and clean and functional. I have more difficulty with the skin itself. I see it become old and ruined. The fine lines blur, the flesh sags and becomes rotten. I see the wrinkles and the scar tissue, the tumours, the sores, the explosions of cancer. I sometimes understand the advantages of leaving an attractive corpse behind.

I phoned the hospital and was told that David was very well and having lots of visitors. I continued to attempt to talk to Libby and at last caught her at home.

She said, 'I've been away.'

'So have I. Derbyshire.'

'I know. I got your message.'

'There's a lot that I couldn't say on the answering machine.'

'Really?'

'Enough to warrant a discussion with you, I'm sure.'

'I'm so busy at the moment.'

I said, 'This is impossible on the telephone. Won't you come round this evening? For drinks? Dinner? Anything you like. Soon. Tonight?'

'All right. Tonight.'

'Does eight suit you?'

She said, 'Fine.'

That evening I put on grey leather slacks and a cream silk shirt in anticipation of Libby's arrival. I bought two veal escalopes and put two bottles of Bollinger in the fridge. By the time she arrived, not very much before midnight, I had drained one of the bottles and was contemplating the second. Libby was flushed, her gait clumsy. She had been drinking heavily. Her normally immaculate face and hair were a mess.

I said, 'Is everything all right?'

'Never better.'

'What went wrong? Why are you so late?'

'You know how it is.'

'No, Libby, I don't.'

'No, you probably don't.'

I said, 'At the very least you might apologise.'

She said, 'I might.'

She looked round the room, saw the neatly set table with its delicate china, its vase of freesias, the champagne flutes and the one empty bottle.

She said, 'It looks like you're nicely set up here for a seduction.'

I could not tell whether this was a taunt or flirtation. Either way I found it rather insulting in the circumstances.

I said, 'You never told me Richard had a son.'

'You don't have to believe everything you hear, do you?'

'I don't think Angelica was lying.'

'Did he have his father's eyes?'

She laughed vulgarly. She slumped on the couch. Her shoes fell off and her eyes slid shut.

I said, 'Where have you been? How did you get in a state like this?'

'I've been with friends, quite a few friends actually.'

She started to cry, very softly at first, then with greater power and volume until she was sobbing uninhibitedly. I crossed the room, knelt beside the couch and stroked her wet cheek. She didn't respond. I did my best to be of comfort. She put out a hand and stroked my head and neck. A shiver of excitement whipped through me. I kissed her on the mouth. She did not object. Her tongue came out to meet mine. I kissed her throat. I ran my hand along her bare back. She pulled up her dress. She was naked beneath. I kissed her breasts.

I said, 'I've waited a long time for this.'

She said, 'I don't know what you were waiting for.'

'Neither do I.'

'I hope it was worth waiting for.'

I was in no doubt that it was. I pulled her gently to her feet and guided her towards the bedroom. She said she needed her handbag though I couldn't imagine why.

I am uncertain how things happened then but I think I must have taken Libby into the bedroom, made her comfortable on the bed, then returned for her handbag. It was open, lying on its side, and some of the contents had spilled out on to the carpet. I picked up the bag and gathered what had fallen out. There were keys, a wallet, and an envelope that contained photographs. For some reason I decided to look at the photographs. Even as I was doing it I knew it was going to be a terrible, terrible mistake. I held them in my hand and they almost burned me.

They showed Libby, naked, surrounded by three naked men. Each had a monstrous erection and was offering it to Libby's mouth. Libby was accepting the offer. I had to look slowly, agonisingly at the image, then I dropped the photographs. I felt physically sick. When I returned to the bedroom Libby was unconscious.

I said, 'You killed him, Libby. I know you did. You may not be a murderess in the eyes of the law, you may not have pulled the trigger but you certainly twisted the knife. You killed Richard. I'm quite sure of that.'

She could not hear me and perhaps if she had been able to hear then I would not have said these words.

I said, 'Richard loved you. Therefore there was nothing for him but suicide. If I'd loved you what else would there have been for me?'

The suicide rate among doctors is high. There are two reasons for this. First, they have easy access to the means of death and they know the correct dosages to ensure perfect results. Secondly, when someone tells them that they have a certain disease (and often they do not need telling) they know precisely how slim the chances are of survival. Unlike the real patients they do not soldier on mouthing tired old consolations to themselves – there's always a chance, doctor – where there's life there's hope – God is merciful – miracles still happen.

I need hardly state that I did not commit suicide. If nothing else, I am not the type.

I'd been sitting too long in the Nevada desert. I'd been pointing my camera and taking Polaroids of nothing in particular – the horizon, the sky, creosote bushes, tumbleweeds, distant blue mountains, tire tracks where previous desert freaks had driven. It was a regular piece of desert, not spectacularly beautiful or spectacularly hostile, and it sure wasn't very photogenic, as my Polaroids were proving. I had run off three or four packs of film. I knew I'd had it for the day. I went back to the hired 4×4 – an unnecessary luxury so far since I didn't have the urge or the nerve to stray very far from the highway. I drove back to where I was staying at the Santiago Inn on the Interstate and was told there had been a call for me from England and could I call back right away.

I didn't know too many people in England but I hoped the call meant work which would mean money, but I didn't know the number and I didn't know the name either – Libby Wisden. I got her answering machine when I first called. The idea of talking to a tape six thousand miles away seemed pretty dumb but I told it I was now back at the hotel and would be there for the rest of the day.

I spread the Polaroids on the bed and gave them a long hard look while I waited, hoping the phone would ring. The desert in the pictures looked fake. The blues were too blue, the reds were too orange. Then the phone rang.

'Hello. Miss Eva Sagendorf?'

'Ms actually, but what the hell.'

'This is Libby Wisden. Thank you for returning my call.'

'That's okay.'

'You don't know me, but you knew my husband.'

'Your husband is?'

'Richard. Richard Wisden.'

'Oh.'

'You remember photographing him.'

'Oh sure.'

'For the cover of his book.'

I guess I did remember, more or less. It was a while ago and it hadn't seemed very important at the time. I had been in London for the summer a few years back and my agent got me a one-off assignment to photograph this Wisden guy for some 'book of the TV series'. I met him at some Elizabethan garden in Lambeth, shot half a dozen rolls of film in thirty minutes, and that was the end of the story. The pictures were good enough for their purpose. I got paid. Richard Wisden had seemed like a nice guy. He asked me to go to a bar with him but I passed on it. I had no idea why his wife should be calling me.

'Richard's dead.'

What do you say? I said, 'Oh, I'm very sorry to hear that, really I am.'

'I've got some photographs that Richard took before he died. They represent the last things he saw. Perhaps if you saw them, you a professional photographer, perhaps you would see something that the untrained eye would probably miss, that the police would certainly miss.'

'Police? How did your husband die?'

'I don't know. That's why I'm ringing you.'

'Huh?'

'There are suspicious circumstances. Murder perhaps.'

'Shit. Okay. Send me the pictures. I guess.'

'They're slides. They're on their way to you now, along with a cheque for five thousand dollars. Is that acceptable?'

'I'll say. But look, what am I supposed to be looking for in these photographs?'

'If I knew that I shouldn't need you at all, should I?'

I said I guessed not. We made a few more polite noises at each other then she rang off. When a woman's just lost her husband and asks you to take a look at a set of his pictures you don't turn her down, however dumb it sounds. When she starts talking about murder and offering you five thousand dollars you know she means business or she's seriously crazy, or maybe both. I hadn't been sure how long I was going to stay at the Santiago Inn but now I knew I had to stick around at least long enough for the transparencies to arrive.

I went out with my camera the next day, not the Polaroid this time. I didn't have high hopes of making great art but I went out all the same because that's what I do. I keep on taking pictures till I come up with something good. I took a lot of less than good pictures that day – more tire tracks crossing and recrossing each other, like they were tying themselves in knots, and concrete highways that headed straight for the vanishing point.

Then I got brave. I left the highway and drove off along a road that wasn't much more than a pair of deep ruts that had been dug by other vehicles. The gradient was gentle at first, then got steeper, the surface getting more corrugated; over the horizon, through a cleft between hills, and down into a dry lake. The desert, of course, had the kind of beauty and vastness that you'd have to be a rock not to be moved and excited by. Sure I was moved and excited but I couldn't see how to translate that into images. Then, suddenly, as I turned round an outcrop of rock, on the top of a ridge maybe a mile and a half away (though distance is pretty hard to judge in the desert) I saw the house.

It was small but outrageous. It had one storey and was made of wood, glass and chrome, dripping with stucco, multicolored mosaics, Greek columns, art deco iron work, crenellations, stained glass, old hub-caps; an accumulation of features, part gothic cathedral, part Spanish castle, part Snow Queen's palace. Yet it didn't look out of place in the desert. It was bizarre enough and extreme enough to stand up for itself. It had to be worth a picture. I drove nearer, stopped the car and took a panoramic view of the house and its surroundings.

I drove nearer some more, stopping once in a while to take more shots. When I got close enough I could see there was a beautiful forties wood-bodied sportster parked in the back of the house. Sure it would never rust in this climate but the sand, the heat and these roads had to be pretty hard on a car out here.

I parked a ways from the house and went to knock on the front door. I didn't know what the etiquette was for paying a visit out here. Maybe you give two weeks' warning that you're on your way. But it seemed I didn't have to worry. As I got to the front door I could see there was someone sitting at one of the windows. It was a man, lean-faced, very black hair, and big dark eyes that looked like they'd seen plenty. Then I saw he was holding an electric guitar. I got near enough for eye contact and he waved for me to come on in the house. I went in. It was small, couldn't have been more than three or four rooms and the man was sitting in the biggest of them. The interior was a lot more restrained than the outside – just simple wooden floors and furniture but set off here and there by a few eye-catching items: a carpet that looked like real zebra, an ornate silver coffee pot, a fifties toy robot in lurid plastics, a gold disc on the wall. The room had an air-conditioner but it was hotter than hell. The man was sitting on a cane chair, nestling a Gibson 335. Behind him there was a stack of battered amplification, and at his feet six, maybe more, effects pedals. There was a permanent hiss from the speakers and once in a while he'd play a flurry of blues scales. The sound was distorted and overcranked but it was obvious he could play.

'Hi,' he said.

'Hi.'

'Do I know you?'

'No,' I said.

'Didn't think I did. Do you know me?'

I shook my head. 'Should I?'

'I guess not. A lot of people used to know me.'

The accent sounded like it had started out English but had taken on a lot of American inflection that left it somewhere in the Atlantic.

'I made some records,' he went on. 'Quite some time ago. You might have heard of me.'

'What's your name?'

'What's yours?' he asked.

'Eva.'

'Nice camera.'

'I'm a photographer. Nice guitar.'

'Yeah. Used to belong to Hendrix. That's what the guy in the store said anyhow, not that you can trust 'em.'

He stomped on a floor pedal and played some more runs that turned into a doomy riff that I knew I'd heard before.

'Remember that one?' he asked.

'Sure. Kinda.'

'Remember the title?'

'No.'

'"Young Suicides".'

'Oh yeah. I've heard of that.'

'Big hit for the Steve Campbell Band. That's me – Steve Campbell.'

Then I remembered. The face was kind of familiar from record sleeves and a couple of televised concerts. He'd aged pretty well. The Steve Campbell Band, as I recalled, played a kind of English rhythm and blues. Campbell had never been a guitar hero but there had been plenty of people who said he was underrated. He'd had some success in the early seventies, made two or three good albums in England, moved to LA and never been heard of since, at least not by me, not that I follow these things very closely these days.

'You'll be glad to know I'm not poised to make a comeback,' he said.

'You live all alone out here?'

'More or less.'

'Must get lonely.'

'Gets lonely everywhere, doesn't it? I got lonely in London. I got lonely as hell in LA.'

'Wild place you've got here,' I said.

'Wouldn't suit everybody but it's home to me.'

'Mind if I photograph it?'

'I don't mind what you do. This is Liberty Hall.'

Outside I began photographing some of the weird architectural detail. On a closer look the mosaics were made of pieces of smashed bottles, car brake lights, fragments of old crockery. The Greek pillar turned out to be made of foam, snatched from some disused film set.

I was discovering all this, taking pictures, minding my own business, wondering what kind of magazine might want to buy pictures of an old rock star's desert retreat, when I realised someone was standing behind me. It was somebody big, much bigger than Steve Campbell. I turned to see who it was and a big male hand grabbed my camera and pulled it away from me. He opened the back, yanked out the film and tossed the camera back to me. I couldn't catch it. It fell to the ground and filled with sand.

'You prick,' I said. 'What did you do that for?'

I was facing a huge guy with the build, looks, and probably all the intelligence and good manners of a gorilla.

He said, 'I felt like it.'

'You fat prick,' I said.

I was aware for a second that the flat of his hand was moving apparently slowly and apparently softly towards my face, but when it hit me it was fast and hard and it was enough to send me sprawling backwards in the sand.

'Don't call me fat,' he said.

We at the Posthumous Society always felt a shade uneasy about sado-masochism, and I have to say I have serious difficulties stating just what my position is on de Sade. I deny all enthusiasm for pain and suffering. I decline to accept any connection between sex and death. The idea that to possess wholly requires the death of the loved one, is an idea that I dismiss as so much 'tosh'.

And yet . . . I do find de Sade interesting and persuasive in his theories about nature. I detect in him a certain childish, call it anal, desire to be bad, to transgress, to be naughty. The desire for destructive sex, violence, poisoning, murder, cannibalism and so forth seems to be an act of daring, a thumbing of the nose at respectable society and at a God who may or may not exist. If God does not exist then 'nature' is supreme, and the divine Marquis finds 'sadism' perfectly natural.

How do I feel about this? Well, I cannot put my hand on my heart and say there is no God. And if there is a God then I suspect he would disapprove of some of the doings of the Posthumous Society. Yet, however riotous, uninhibited, or 'unrestrained' events became at our meetings I never felt any sense of transgression, and I certainly never felt I was doing anything 'unnatural'.

I would be happy to debate the matter. I wish we'd discussed this sort of issue more often at our meetings, but there was little call for it from the other members. They always told me I experienced sex too much 'in the head'. I suggested that this is precisely where we all experience it. I suggested that the body is merely a lot of pleasure centres that tell the brain what a good time it's having. I was indeed looking forward to an evening alone with Libby Wisden, and perhaps the pleasure of anticipation is indeed a cerebral one.

She arrived looking less glamorous than she had for the initiation, yet one could certainly not complain. I had organised a little light refreshment and the dining table at my flat was groaning with the archives of the Posthumous Society. The archives consist of application forms along with the head-and-shoulder 'mug shots' that first accompanied those forms. Then there is a letters file, subscription details, a mailing list, a reading list, and a considerable number of albums of Polaroids showing the society's activities. These include the famous initiation portraits.

· These archives, and especially the photograph albums, can provide considerable entertainment if browsed casually, but Libby wanted to go through them all systematically and humourlessly. I soon realised I was in for a long and not very erotic evening.

'All these people,' said Libby. 'Who'd have thought it? Did Richard make love to all these people?'

'Not the men,' I replied.

'But all the women? All of them?'

'I never kept records of precisely who did what with whom and how many times, but most of them, yes.'

'How about this one?'

She had stopped at a photograph of an attractive if slightly 'tarty' young woman whom I knew was called Trudy.

'As a matter of fact,' I said, 'Richard introduced her to the Posthumous Society himself.'

'Did he indeed?'

'I hope this isn't going to be too painful for you?' I said, but Libby did not look pained.

I admitted that Trudy had been one of our minor 'mistakes'. Richard's recommendation had made me a little less thorough in considering her application. A fancy-dress party was arranged for one of the first meetings she attended. She and Richard both came naked but for a few strategic bunches of herbs. It was applauded wildly at the time. Trudy had a necklace of mints and sages, a waistband of thymes, rue and angelica leaves in her hair, a garland of French parsley intertwined in her pubic hair, and a rose between her teeth.

She was a great favourite with all and sundry. She made a lot of friends at that meeting, but the friendship wore a little thin when everyone who had had 'contact' with Trudy came down with a rather virulent attack of crabs.

'I should think it was a recurring problem,' said Libby.

'It most certainly was not,' I said.

'Lucky it wasn't something worse.'

I would not be drawn on that subject. Libby then came across several photographs of Richard in 'group situations'. She stared very intently at one of these as though she was trying to identify someone in the group.

Then, quite out of the blue, she said, 'You must have made a lot of money out of Richard over the years.'

'I beg your pardon?' I snapped.

87

'Perhaps not you personally, but the bank – all the loans Richard had with you to finance his business, all the interest and the bank charges. It must have added up over the years.'

I was completely taken aback but I managed to retort, 'Those loans enabled him to make a small fortune for himself. He made a lot of money out of us.'

'That's another thing I've never understood,' she said. 'How did Richard manage to get a loan from you in the first place? The other banks had turned him down flat. He had no security. He had precious little experience.'

'Not all banks are afraid of taking a small risk,' I said. 'I saw that Richard had great potential. I thought he was a "good risk". My decision was vindicated.'

'Even so I would have thought . . .'

'Libby,' I said, 'you came here to discover one or two little secrets about the Posthumous Society. Confidential banking information is another matter.'

She smiled. I turned to putty in her hands.

'Who is this man?' she asked, turning her attention to the albums again.

'Offhand I don't know.'

'Look a little more closely,' she said.

'It's difficult. It's taken from a rather unusual angle.'

I did know of course. It was Sir Leonard Anderson, our only ever knighted member. It was possible that Libby might have recognised him from pictures in the press. He was frequently having his photograph on the cover of business magazines, and yet I wondered if she had special motives for singling him out of the crowd. I clammed up. She did not press me further.

It was after midnight before she had finished her survey of the archives. We went to my bedroom and performed, I would have to admit, a rather perfunctory act of 'union'. Probably we were both to blame. It did not take long.

Afterwards I said, 'Libby dear, you said you wanted to know why Richard died, and you said you thought I could tell you.'

'Did I say that? I think I was only referring to the files.'

'I'm sorry if you didn't find what you were looking for.'

'Didn't I?'

'Did you?'

She would not answer my question. She was out of bed before I could probe further. She dressed and gave me a kiss that at its most charitable could have been called 'sisterly', and she was gone leaving me with a warm bed and a large pile of disarrayed files as well as a full measure of postcoital sadness.

I had too the distinct impression that I would not be graced by Libby Wisden's presence again. She had got what she came for and had no reason to come again. It was only later that I realised she had absconded with a number of photographs.

She was pretty and not all that old and she sat on the chair next to my hospital bed. She sat really close and I could smell her. It was perfume. It was quite strong and I don't normally like that, but this was very nice.

'I've wanted to meet you for a long time, David,' she said.

'Oh?' I said.

'Richard would never let me meet you. Your mother wasn't keen on the idea either. I can't really blame them. How's your leg?'

'It's nothing,' I said. 'I don't know why they're keeping me here.'

'How did it happen?'

She wasn't going to get round me.

'It was an accident. I was playing with a shotgun. I knew I shouldn't have been. My mother had told me a thousand times.'

I wasn't sure if she believed me. She looked as though she

did but I didn't know who she'd been talking to. I didn't know which side she was on. So I asked her.

'Which side are you on?'

'I beg your pardon, David?'

She was playing dumb, but we can all play that little game.

'What do you know about the water-pistols?' I asked.

That threw her. She obviously knew something about them but she wasn't telling. She seemed surprised that I knew.

'What do *you* know about them?'

'I'm asking the questions,' I said.

'Are you indeed?'

'Yes.'

She gave me one of those smiles that adults give you when they think they're being so clever, so superior. It says, 'I know it all and you're just a kid.' It put my back up straight away.

'What questions do you want to ask me?' she said, all smiles.

'My dad? Is he really dead?'

'Why do you ask that?'

'I've only heard it from my mother and she's not very reliable.'

'Is she not? Why not?'

'She drinks too much, and she messes about with drugs . . . but I asked you a question.'

'Yes, you did. Yes, Richard is dead, I'm afraid.'

She said it really sadly, really sincerely, but I don't know how you can tell when it's genuine. Adults, they're buggers.

'How did he die?'

'There you have me, David. There is an official version that seems to be regarded as sufficient for police, the newspapers, the inquest, for a private detective. This version says he was depressed . . .'

'What does depressed mean exactly?'

'It means when you're really fed up.'

'Okay.'

'And your father, my husband, is supposed to have taken his own life using a combination of drink and sleeping tablets. I'm not sure if you and I really accept that, eh David?'

She was cleverer than I'd expected. She knew what I'd been thinking about.

She went on, 'I think he may have been murdered.'

'Wow! Who by?'

'I don't know, David. That's why I came to see you. But you're asking the questions.'

This was amazing. I hadn't ever done anything like an interrogation before. I didn't know where to start.

'Do you have a job?' I asked.

'Yes.'

'What?'

'A peculiar sort of job. I'm a food critic.'

'It sounds really strange to me.'

'To me too sometimes.'

'Do you think my dad was in a secret organisation?'

'I don't know. Was he?'

'I think he must have been,' I said. 'I don't know who they are but I have one or two ideas. They have the water-pistol as their secret sign. Johnny Fantham had one. Do you know Johnny Fantham?'

'He was working for me.'

'Was he? Was he? And that lady doctor. Was she working for you?'

'In a sense.'

'And the girl who brought the car to the house?'

'I don't know anything about her, I'm afraid.'

'I wonder where she fits in?' I said. 'And my mother, is she with us or against us? What about all the people who came to the house?'

'Perhaps that's where the answer lies.'

She was clever, too clever for me really, not that I claim to be as clever as all that. Somehow I found I was telling her all these things, about the goings-on at Woodbine Cottage that I probably shouldn't have been telling her.

'Would you recognise any of the people again?'

'Some of them, I'm sure.'

She had some photographs with her, just faces, just heads and shoulders. They were men and women of all different ages. One or two looked like they might be criminals but most

91

of them looked pretty ordinary. There weren't any children.

'Are you with the police?' I said.

'No.'

'Where did these pictures come from?'

'From a friend of mine called Basil.'

'That's a funny name. Why did he have the photographs?'

She shrugged. She pushed the photographs along the bed and I looked at the faces again.

'Are these people wanted by the police or something?'

'No.'

'Are they members of a secret society?'

She smiled and I knew I'd got it right, that I'd been right all along.

'Are you a member of this society?' I asked.

'In a way.'

'Is Johnny Fantham a member?'

'No.'

'Do you think one of these people murdered my dad?'

'It's possible, isn't it?'

It was really nice to be with an adult who treated you decently and didn't behave like they knew everything.

'What are the aims of this secret society?' I asked her.

'Oh, pleasure, staying young, keeping death at bay.'

I knew what pleasure was. I couldn't see why anybody would want to stay young. Being young's just a pain in the bum as far as I can see. They always say it's the happiest days of your life. I hope not. I couldn't see how joining a club could keep you young unless it was something really weird, like messing about with hormones and things, not that I know what hormones are, anyway. I didn't tell her I didn't understand. I just looked at the pictures.

I said, 'These aren't the sort of people who came to Woodbine Cottage. The people who came to the house always looked a bit scruffy. I think some of them must have been drug addicts. They never came when my dad was there. Well, he'll never be there now, will he? What if they were really scared of him so they got rid of him so now they can come to the house whenever they like?

'And this girl who brought the car. I don't know who she

was and I don't know why she brought the car, but there was something in the boot. It looked like a lot of letters – secret messages, something like that. Didn't Johnny Fantham tell you what they were?'

'No, he didn't.'

'Then he must have had his reasons.'

'No doubt.'

'What kind of secret messages, I wonder?'

'About ways of keeping death at bay, perhaps.'

'Yes,' I agreed, although I didn't know what she really meant. Still, she seemed well satisfied with the explanation so I just nodded and tried to look intelligent.

'David,' she said, 'you've been an enormous help. Richard's estate will take a certain amount of sorting out but I'm sure there'll be something in it for you.'

I didn't know what that meant either but she seemed to think I should be pleased so I tried to look pleased. A nurse came by and started taking my pulse and temperature so Libby Wisden went away. She gave me a kiss and that was very nice. She also gave me a phone number where I could ring her if I thought of anything else.

It seemed to me she was a lot too easily satisfied, but I had the last laugh because I *had* recognised one of the faces in the photographs. He was quite old and he had a moustache and he had the kind of hair that's black in some places and snow white in others, and on the back of the photograph there was the name 'Anderson'. He'd been to Woodbine Cottage a few times. He seemed to be one of the ones wanting money and he dressed very smartly and he drove a Mercedes. I hadn't told Libby Wisden that I recognised him because sometimes you've got to play your cards close to your chest in this game and sometimes the female can be deadlier than the male.

It was a good day for visitors. My mother came in the early evening and of course I didn't say anything about Libby. She, my mother, brought me some fruit and some comics and she left quite early. It wasn't as if we had very much to say to each other. She said she was sorry about my leg and I said I forgave her.

Then after she'd gone, just as visiting time was nearly over

I had another visitor. Was I glad to see him. It was Johnny Fantham. He was wearing a leather jacket and he looked really tough.

'All right, kid?' he said.

'Yes,' I said. 'I've got a lot to tell you.'

'I've got plenty to tell you as well.'

'Tell me then.'

'Not here. Not now. We've got to get you out of here and fast. You're in a lot of danger.'

It was the most exciting thing I'd ever heard.

'Sorry I had to do that,' the gorilla said.

I picked myself up.

'You didn't have to do anything,' I said. 'Ever hear of free will?'

'You shouldn't have called me fat is all. And no photographs. Okay? See?'

'Okay. I see. There were easier ways you could have made me see.'

'Pick up your camera, get back in your Jeep and beat it.'

'You know this camera is probably ruined for good,' I said.

'Give me your address. We'll send you a check.'

'I'm not dumb enough to give you my address, asshole!'

'It's your decision.'

'Yeah, it is.'

I got back in the four by four and headed back to the highway and the Santiago Inn. I'd always known there was all kinds of weirdness in the desert, burned out guitarists, fat guys who thought they were Clint Eastwood, but maybe I was lucky not to have found someone who thought he was Manson or Son of Sam or Jesus Christ. There's room to hide a whole lot of corpses out there in the Nevada desert.

94

'Package for you, Miss Sagendorf.'

The girl on the desk, whose name tag said she was called Rosemary, handed me Richard Wisden's transparencies. They'd arrived by courier while I was out. It was a small box of Ektachrome slides. They looked like originals, in which case I hoped his wife had a set of dupes. I didn't want all that responsibility for the last things a dead man saw. I held them to the light but that didn't tell me much. I went to the local camera store, showed them my sandy camera. They were full of sympathy but they'd have to send the camera away. That was no good to me. But they could rent me a projector.

I schlepped back to my room with it, set it up and gave myself a slide show. It wasn't a whole lot more interesting than a lot of boring slide shows I'd seen before.

The first slide showed the patio of a modern house. From the architectural style and the quality of the light it had to be English. The building was red brick with a lot of windows and a lot of plants. You could see that most of the plants were herbs. I could make out fennel, some chives, lavender.

The second slide showed a wrecked car – a white Jaguar without wheels or doors or windows. It was resting on a patch of ground that was a mess of red mud, broken glass and bricks. Tall weeds formed a background along a wire fence. The car looked like some terminally ill animal, dying yet still dangerous and prepared to fight for its last stand.

Slide three: a green headland pointing out to sea, like a finger indicating the pale orange sunset. Just another sunset picture.

Slide four: a woman's torso – pale, plump, heavy blue veins in the breasts. Legs and face were out of the picture. It was lit by watery grey light filtering through a window offstage left. Libby Wisden's torso? How would I know? I never met the woman.

The fifth slide showed a shop window, a joke shop. There were lots of small tacky items – green rubber snakes, plastic skulls, farting cushions. The sidewalk in front of the store was wet with rain and there was the blur of a moving male figure on the right edge of the picture.

Slide six was a room, just an empty English 'living room'. The furniture looked expensive. There were modern art prints on the walls, though nothing I recognised. The carpet looked Persian. The floor was parquet. There was a coffee table with a pile of glossies and a vase of tulips. How could anyone live with all that good taste?

Slide seven: the interior of a restaurant, possibly Italian, though the shot was taken with camera-mounted flash and hadn't lit all the room. A waiter was standing in the center of the restaurant, a carafe of wine in one hand, his other hand shielding his face from the camera.

The eighth slide was a self-portrait of Richard Wisden. The man himself. The last picture of the dead man? The face was mostly obscured by the camera which he was pointing into the mirror, but you could see that the chin was sweaty and unshaven. You could see that the hands were dirty. I guess he'd been gardening.

Slide nine: a square patch of bare earth – dark, rich, fertile looking. Some kind of complex geometric design had been drawn on the earth using chalk or white sand – interlocking lines and semicircles.

Slide ten: an English railway line. The picture was taken from a bridge above the tracks. The tracks ran straight, almost to the horizon, then they got tangled up with points and crossings, and started tangling and multiplying.

Slide eleven: an English skyscraper, photographed from street level, pushing up into a bright blue sky with a few flecks of soft, white cloud. The building was mostly glass and reflected that sky. I thought of a chameleon, as though the building was trying to blend in with its surroundings. Along the bottom edge of the frame you could see the name Anderson set out on the building in big, plain, stainless steel letters.

Slide twelve: an English roofscape – cramped inner-city houses, a hundred different brick and tile colors, clean but complex geometry, cut with television aerials and phone lines.

Slide thirteen: a wide English street on a winter's day, packed with people. If I had to guess I'd say it was Oxford Street, London, but there must be other streets that look like that. All the people looked bland and anonymous. The photograph didn't compose itself round any one person or group of people. There was one guy wearing a bowler hat. There was a woman in a big red, shaggy fur coat, but you could easily have singled out other 'interesting' people.

That was all. Did they mean anything? Not to me. I'd hate to sound like a junior professor at some third-rate city college, but the biggest task facing a photographer is not to make his or her pictures 'mean' anything, but to let them 'be'. One problem with that line of thought was that, so far as I knew, Richard Wisden didn't think of himself as a photographer at all, so maybe he did intend them to 'mean' something.

The pictures were taken with a fairly good 35mm camera, but everybody has one of those these days. Some of them didn't seem much more than snapshots (the living room, the patio, the restaurant, the patch of earth); others seemed to be consciously trying to be good pictures (the store window, the wrecked car, the self-portrait) – the kind of stuff that gets into first-year photography students' portfolios; others just seemed downright 'nothingy' (the street scene, the railway lines, the Anderson building).

You'd be inclined to say they were pictures anybody might take, but not just anybody did. Richard Wisden did and he was dead. In your average murder mystery one of the diners in the restaurant would be the same as one of the people in the street scene, his name would be Anderson, the nude torso would belong to his girlfriend and she'd be the one who crashed the Jaguar.

Or maybe the plot of earth has a corpse in it. The murder was done in the tasteful English room. The body was taken by train to a headland that has ordinary sunsets. The murderer turns out to be the owner of the joke shop.

Yes, sure, pictures can have those sort of meanings and maybe that was what Libby Wisden wanted to hear from me. For five thousand dollars she was entitled to hear anything she wanted.

Then the phone. 'Miss Sagendorf. It's Rosemary here on the desk. There's a Mr Campbell here to see you.'

'Here?'

'At the desk.'

'Oh shit. Tell him I'll be down in a while.'

'If you could hurry, Miss Sagendorf. He seems kind of impatient.'

What did that mean? I switched off the projector, left the transparencies in the magazine, picked up my Polaroid camera, locked the hotel room and went to the lobby.

Steve Campbell was leaning on the reception desk. He had to lean to stop himself falling. He was on something and he was flying. I could hear he was having a very loud discussion with Rosemary about Muzak. He had a point. At that very moment a Tijuana arrangement of early Lennon and McCartney songs was bleeding round the lobby.

'Shit,' he said to the girl, 'how can you work with this kind of musical junk in your ears all day? This is music to slash your wrists by.'

'It's company policy, I think.'

'I've got some tapes I could give you to play. Good stuff. Really.'

'I'd love to hear it, but you know, the management . . .'

Then he saw me. He shut up and looked embarrassed. I thought he was the kind of guy who didn't look embarrassed too often.

'I owe you a big apology,' he said.

'*You* don't but your pet ape does.'

'That's Harry. He's okay.'

'Oh really?'

He pulled a wad of frayed-looking bills from his pocket and pressed them into my hand. I tried not to take hold but he closed his fingers round mine so I had to.

'Do you want to go for a drive?'

'No thanks.'

'Have you seen my car?'

'Yes.'

'It's class, isn't it?'

'It's fine, but you see I don't want your money, and I don't want to go driving with you. I just want you to leave me alone.'

'But you want to take some pictures. Come back to the house and take some more pictures.'

98

'And get another camera destroyed? No thanks.'

'Harry's okay but you shouldn't have called him a fat prick.'

'I didn't call him a fat prick till after he'd broke my camera.'

A couple of mid-West businessmen in leisure suits and expensive sunglasses were staring kind of intently at us. I couldn't blame them. Steve Campbell was quite a spectacle and he was talking very loud. The words "fat prick" disturbed these two guys strangely and I heard them tut-tutting under their breath, and then muttering something about 'teaching that guy some manners'. Steve Campbell heard this as well as I did and it seemed to make him lose what little cool he still had.

'Hey you guys, I said "fat prick". That seems to disturb you. Is it just the words? Or is it the concept? How do you feel about the thing itself?'

He was well on the way to exposing himself but I grabbed him by the arm, led him out of the hotel and told him I was just dying to take a ride in his car.

It was so easy to get out of the hospital. You wouldn't believe how easy it was. Johnny Fantham left the ward. I pretended to go to the loo. I was limping a bit but nobody seemed to notice, then I slipped out when nobody was looking. I met Johnny by the stairs. He gave me a coat to put on. We went down in the lift. Nobody stopped us. We went to his car.

'This is great,' I said. 'Where are we going?'

'London.'

'That's great. I've never been there.'

'It's overrated,' he said.

He didn't say very much else. I don't think detectives usually do. He didn't seem very happy. He drove quite fast but it was an old car. We had the radio on. It was just pop

99

music. He had it on very loud. It got dark. We were on the motorway. It was exciting.

'Do you believe in eternal life?' I asked.

'What?'

I asked him again.

'What, heaven and hell?'

'Sort of.'

'Pays not to think about it.'

'But this secret society,' I said, 'the one with the water-pistols . . .'

'What are you talking about?'

'It was something Libby Wisden said.'

'When did you talk to that cow?'

'Earlier today.'

He looked really puzzled about that. He said he didn't like the sound of that. I told him he didn't have to worry. I said I hadn't given anything away, although I did wonder if I'd said too much to Libby Wisden. But I wanted to tell him my theory. It was still only a theory at this stage.

'This society,' I said, 'I think they could be working on trying to give people immortality, sort of tampering with nature.'

'Do me a favour,' he said.

'What sort of favour?'

He shook his head.

'I know it sounds fantastic.'

'What society is this you're talking about?'

That's when I started to get suspicious. Libby Wisden had said that Johnny Fantham wasn't a member, but he'd had the water-pistol. How come, when he claimed he didn't know which society we were talking about? Then he'd had the car key and he'd taken away the evidence. Why?

'What did you find in the boot of that car?' I asked.

'Never you mind.'

'But I do mind.'

'Then mind your own business instead.'

'Was it secret messages?'

'Anybody ever tell you you've got too much imagination, kid?'

100

That really did it. I didn't like that. I didn't like the way he called me 'kid'. And how can you have too much imagination?

'Why did you have the key to the boot, anyway?'

'I don't owe you any explanations, kid. Understand?'

'Why was I in danger? Who from? Where are you taking me?'

'I told you. London. Now pipe down.'

'I don't like this.'

'Nobody cares what you like.'

'Who are you working for?'

'I shan't tell you again. Pipe down.'

I piped down all right. I didn't say a thing for the next hour. He tried to make conversation every so often but I wasn't having any of that. I was fed up. I'd thought Johnny Fantham was a really good bloke but now I wasn't so sure. He didn't seem to know anything. He knew less than I did, and he wouldn't even tell me what he *did* know. I thought we were on the same side. I thought we should pool our knowledge. Maybe he was really a bad guy. Maybe he was on the other side. I started to think I could be being kidnapped. I got a bit scared. I got very scared really. We were going seventy-five miles an hour. I couldn't jump out of the car. I felt cold. My leg hurt. The radio was on too loud. I started crying.

'What are you crying about?'

'I'm not crying. I'm fed up. I'm depressed. I want my mother.'

'Yeah? Well she doesn't want you.'

I got really mad at that. I knew that wasn't true. She might not be the perfect mother but she cared about me really. I got really mad that he'd say a thing like that. I grabbed the steering wheel and pulled it as hard as I could. It gave Johnny Fantham a bit of a shock. We were in the middle lane and we shot to the left across the slow lane. We nearly hit a lorry. The car went on to the hard shoulder, all screeching and swerving as he tried to get it back under control. He managed. He did an emergency stop. We were thrown all over the place. He pulled the handbrake on and switched on the flashing lights. Then he hit me across the face with the back of his hand. My head hit the side window.

'That didn't hurt,' I said.

'The next one will,' he said and he held up his hand to threaten me.

'No it won't,' I said. 'You're weak and you're a coward and you're no bloody good.'

I could have been cleverer. Instead of arguing I could have leapt out of the car and run away. But I didn't. I was too slow and I couldn't have run very fast. He started driving again but much slower this time. I'd got him rattled.

'I know I'm no bloody good,' he said.

That really surprised me. It's not the sort of thing adults say, especially not detectives, I should think.

'I've got a kid myself,' he went on. 'A little girl. Diane. She's about your age. I don't see much of her. She lives with her mother. Look, I don't feel good about this, you know. I feel rotten, but I've got to do it. There's no way I can't.'

'*What* have you got to do?'

'I've got to deliver you to a certain party in London.'

'I don't like parties.'

'A bloke. Some geezer called Anderson.'

'Why have you *got* to do it?'

'They'll hurt my little girl if I don't.'

'What about them hurting me?'

He had to think about that. He didn't answer for a long time. I could see his face. He looked really scared. He looked really scared and stupid – just like all the others.

'I mean,' he said, 'blood's thicker than water.'

I thought he *is*, he *is* just like all the others. I'm cleverer than he is. I can beat him. I can probably beat him with one hand behind my back, with one leg in bandages.

'I understand,' I said. 'You've got to do what you've got to do. It's all right.'

'I'm glad you understand, kid.'

'We're still friends aren't we?' I said.

'Of course,' he said. 'I mean of course we're friends.'

He was thick as two short planks. We passed a road sign that said there were services in eight miles. I said I wanted something to eat, and because he thought we were still friends he said all right. We got to the services and parked. I said I didn't think I could make it into the cafeteria because my leg was hurting. That worried him a bit. So he went to buy me a sandwich and left me in the car. He also left his keys in the ignition. He really wasn't very bright. My dad had showed me how to drive. I wasn't very good but I didn't need to be very good for what I had in mind.

I got into the driver's seat and I got the engine going. I needed both hands to get the handbrake off. I couldn't find the switch for the lights but that didn't really matter. I put the car into gear and set off. The car leapt about three feet in the air but it didn't stall. It shot forward, hit one car, bounced off, scraped along the side of two other cars, crashed into the back of a van and stopped.

It worked just like I'd planned it to. People came running. They were shouting. There were police and lorry drivers, a man from the RAC, even a nurse in uniform. It was great.

'What happened? Are you all right, lad?'

'I'm very well thank you,' I said.

'Who are you with? Are you with your mum and dad?'

'My dad's dead,' I said.

'He's in his pyjamas.'

'Who *are* you with then?'

I could see that Johnny Fantham had come running out when he'd heard the crash. He was standing on the edge of the crowd. He didn't know whether to come over or run for it. I felt a bit sorry for him. Then the nurse saw I'd got one of those plastic tags round my wrist that they'd put on in hospital. She pointed it out to a policeman.

'There's something very funny going on around here,' somebody said.

I pointed at Johnny Fantham. He was still standing there. He hadn't run. He didn't move and everybody looked at him. He looked really old and stooped, and very stupid holding a sandwich. He looked like he was going to cry. Soft bugger.

'Yes, there is something funny going on, officer,' I said, 'but I can explain . . .'

103

Richard used to say to me, 'Trudy, you and me, we're two of a kind', which was absolutely untrue because he was a Piscean and that was his main problem. I wouldn't want to be a Piscean. Oh yes they're sensitive and artistic, spiritual, all that, but they're also like two fishes swimming in opposite directions.

The Piscean traits are sensitivity, imagination, psychic ability and compassion, but if they're not careful they can become timid, idle dreamers with no will of their own. Just look at some of the famous Pisceans – Einstein, Michelangelo, Nureyev, Liz Taylor, Harold Wilson.

But she, Libby, was a Scorpion. Famous Scorpions include Charles Atlas, Indira Gandhi, Art Garfunkel and Rock Hudson. I think that shows the difference pretty clearly.

Scorpions have drive, charisma and self-confidence, but that can turn so easily into ruthlessness, suspicion and sadism.

Look at sex. The Piscean is given to intrigues, secret meetings, all that. They can be a bit kinky though Richard wasn't especially, though it all depends what you mean by kinky. Scorpions regard sex more like a keep-fit class. They're physically uninhibited but they're mentally suspicious and they can be frightened emotionally.

Scorpio woman with Pisces man can be a very good combination because they have a 5-9 sun sign pattern. They have the ability to communicate without words and I think that's beautiful. And that can go on after death as well!! Let's face it, life and death are just different astral levels. The fact that one half of a couple is on a different level doesn't mean the couple have to lose touch with one another.

The Scorpio appears to be the strong one, the decision-maker. The Pisces appears to be the drifter, the one who goes with the tide. Yet in a Pisces/Scorpio relationship it's usually the Piscean who wields most power. The Scorpion may appear to be all calm and in control but underneath there can be a shocking turmoil. I think that was really true of Libby.

One thing that's really typical Scorpion is wanting to know 'the truth beyond the truth'. That applies to religion, politics, human relationships, everything. When Richard died it was natural enough that she should look for something behind the obvious facts. I tried to help her as much as I could but she wasn't easy to help.

The Piscean man is always searching for the 'real thing' emotionally. However, all too often the search becomes an end in itself. He can be so busy searching that he misses the real thing when it comes along.

So he used to say we were two of a kind and that we were both looking for something but we didn't know what. I always said I knew exactly what I was looking for and it certainly wasn't the man of my dreams.

I've been in this game a while now but I don't hate men. I don't think they're all scum. I don't think sex is about hatred for all of them, in fact I know it's not, but it is for some of them. It seems like they could all have it inside them somewhere but most of them manage to keep it under control. You see I don't believe in sin but I do think it's a crime against nature to squander the precious life force. I don't think I'm wasting mine but I think a lot of men are wasting theirs.

Richard was different. He wasn't *totally* different. He was a punter before he was anything else, and that's another thing about Pisceans, sometimes they can be really generous and sometimes they can be really mean depending on their mood.

I don't know why but for some reason I thought Richard might be really strange sexually, but he wasn't. He liked to take a few pictures but there's nothing wrong with that. Then he took me along to these orgies organised by his bank manager. I thought the bank manager was a funny sod, but that's another story. I don't know what sign he was. I'm a Leo, that's part lion and part pussycat.

Richard had some really interesting ideas about plants. I've always hated gardening. I think because my father's so bloody keen. I thought Richard would just be into bedding plants and weed killers but he was better than that. He told me how in olden days every plant was assigned to a different part of the zodiac, which is logical when you think about it. He gave me three little pots of herbs. They were parsley, caraway, and winter savoury. I looked them up in a herbal and it turned out that all three were under Mercury. If that wasn't enough, just before he died Richard sent me to this place in Derbyshire called Woodbine Cottage. Woodbine is also under the influence of Mercury! How about that?

Richard was interested in folk tales and that kind of thing. In mythology, he said, and even in fairy tales a plant is often used as a way of entering a magical world. I've never been involved with drugs because it seems to me that in my business you have enough problems without developing any expensive habits; but I've read Castenada and I've heard about magic mushrooms and all that stuff, but Richard said even something really innocent-seeming like Jack and the Beanstalk showed it as well.

Then a long while after Richard's death I got a visit from Libby Wisden. I don't know how she got my address, whether it was that bastard Fantham at the hotel or whether she'd found it in with Richard's things.

I didn't take to her at all. She seemed the worst sort of Scorpio – cold, suspicious, difficult, determined to give everybody a hard time, but at least she didn't try and smarm me.

'I want to know how and why my husband died.'

'Do you?'

'And you can help me.'

'Can I?'

'I think so.'

'Well you're absolutely right. I know exactly how and why Richard died.'

She looked white as a sheet. That was typical. There she was making trouble but as soon as the truth was within her grasp she was terrified.

'I'll tell you,' I said. 'But it'll cost.'

106

The photographs which Libby had 'purloined' were in fact perfectly decorous and proper ones. They were the head and shoulders photographs which had accompanied initial applications to the Posthumous Society. They did not seem to constitute a liability. On the other hand I would look extremely silly if I could not even keep such a basic part of the archives safe. Yet, whatever use Libby had in mind for them, one simple phone call followed by one short visit ought to be enough to secure their return, and I determined I would do that first thing tomorrow.

It was, however, impossible to reach Libby. I kept ringing her number only to find myself chatting with an answering machine. The absence of the photographs allied to Libby's elusiveness did, I admit, give me a little concern – oh, not a great worry, it felt like a tedious errand I needed to complete before I could be completely at ease.

The aspect that interested me most was that Libby had made special mention of Trudy and Sir Leonard Anderson. Trudy was no problem – a lively little wench, unhygienic perhaps but hardly significant. Sir Leonard was a much bigger fish – a distinguished businessman, property developer, benefactor, orgiast, yet perfectly respectable and above board. Did Libby believe these two held some clue to her husband's death? Was she, for all I knew, correct? I think not.

I had a theory about Richard's death. It was not a very original theory, but it did, I thought, have the advantage of being correct. Let me explain.

One needs to consider again the curious connection between love, sex, pain and death. I hope this does not sound too heavy.

Richard, like myself, found that marriage was not enough for him. He does seem to have chosen a spouse who was very badly matched, yet it might well have been the same whoever he had married. He wanted an excess of pleasure, sensuality, sex and lust. Most men do. Richard pursued that excess through the auspices of the Posthumous Society.

I was frequently tempted to draw up a list of 'tenets' for the Posthumous Society but could find nobody with whom to share the task. If I had to state what our aims were I should say they were the pursuit of happiness and pleasure and the affirmation of life. You will find those who will argue (feminists I suppose) that male sexuality is the manifestation of a death-based culture. Well, there's no arguing with people like that, is there?

So yes, we were on the side of life. We tore our pleasures. We did not go gentle. We live, all of us, in an age which is reluctant, nay afraid, to experience the grand emotions; but some of us are not afraid, or at least did not used to be. I was never foolish enough to believe that sexual excess is any sort of charm against mortality, but by God it made me feel alive while I was enjoying it.

Look at the eighteenth century. Anyone who was the slightest jot promiscuous knew, with almost absolute certainty, that they were going to contract syphilis. They were going to suffer from nerve disorders, skin disease, loss of teeth, atrophy of the bones, blindness, madness and death. And did eighteenth-century men and women resolve to be celibate, chaste or monogamous? Indeed they did not. They may have been racked with fear. They may have taken the odd precaution (ineffective), and the occasional cure (usually worse than the disease), but they still needed to feel the rush of pleasure and life, even if feeling it hastened the approach of death.

AIDS of course is today's 'nightmare', yet there are two things of which we may be certain: one, it will not mean an end of sexual adventurism, and two, a cure will be found. This latter may take some time (and I realise this is no comfort to those already dying from the disease) but it will be sooner rather than later.

The decline and eventual death of the Posthumous Society was, perhaps, inevitable in these days of creeping 'Victorian' values and demands for 'safe' sex. Who wants sex to be safe? Sex demands the thrill of danger, the whiff of sulphur, the rattle of the winged chariot. This is my belief and I am not alone in it.

What does this have to do with Richard Wisden? This: Richard was a libertine, a hedonist, a sybarite, call it what you will. His wife would not go along with this so he found excitement and satisfaction by joining the Posthumous Society. But he only found those things for so long.

There is an important question at stake here, and it is a question to which I have no dogmatic answer. The question is: does one inevitably begin by being satisfied with one partner, then inevitably become bored, curious, dissatisfied with that one partner? Does one then inevitably seek a new partner, several new partners? Does one then need tens, dozens, scores? Does this too inevitably become tedious? Does this lead to a slide into fetishism, to bizarre sex, to perversions that veer ever closer to imitations of death?

I am sure there are no hard and fast rules, yet I find this a persuasive model. Certainly at the last few meetings of the Posthumous Society Richard was listless, unhappy, aggressive, drew no pleasure from the proceedings and consistently failed to sport an erection.

This may have been partly due to tiredness, anxiety and excessive drinking, but I think it was more the fact that the pleasures on offer failed to excite him. Like any sort of addict he needed a bigger kick. What sort of kick? I don't know. Coprophilia, necrophilia? Who can say? However, I think I can say that it seemed to Richard that if he could no longer derive any pleasure from sexuality in whatever form, then the time had come to end it all.

I could have tried to tell Libby my theory but I did not. I think she would not have accepted it. On the evidence of her behaviour at the two meetings I had witnessed she derived no particular pleasure from sex, yet she did not see this as a reason to commit suicide. Perhaps that weakened my theory but I still thought it was true in Richard's case. Certainly I didn't think there was any more convincing truth to be found

109

in the Posthumous Society archives, in a few stolen head and shoulders photographs.

I never did get them back and after a while I stopped worrying and after that ceased to care at all. In fact I have never seen Libby Wisden from that day till this.

A very long time later, when I had lost all interest in the death of Richard Wisden, not that I was ever overwhelmed with interest, I received an odd and somewhat alarming invitation that brought it all back to me. The invitation was delivered by hand, had a black border to it, and said in embossed lettering:

You are invited to the Regent Room at the Hancock Hotel at 8 p.m. on March 13th when you will learn something to your advantage concerning the death of Richard Wisden.

Dear Libby,
I hope you will not mind me writing to you out of the blue like this. I hope you will not think I am imposing on personal grief, though I suppose there's no other kind of grief, actually. I know that at times like this words are often useless but perhaps they can also be a comfort.

Well then, let me begin by expressing my sincerest condolences. Yes, your grief is your own but you're not alone in it. Lots of us out here in 'televisionland' share your sad loss.

I have been a fan (terrible word) of Richard's since I can't remember when, yet I've always thought of myself as more than that, just as I have always thought of Richard as more than just a TV presenter and gardener. I have thought of him as a friend and a good companion. I have invited him into my home and he has been a very welcome guest. Although I was never able to meet my hero in person I feel sure that we would have become fast friends if that happy encounter had taken place.

I always meant to write to poor Richard while he was alive and ask for a signed photograph, but somehow I never found the time. Also I'm rather a shy person by nature, and now it is too late to send a 'fan' letter. Or is it?

Firstly my letter may be some comfort to you, his dear widow, but also I feel that somewhere up there Richard is still watching us and is aware of these words.

Sometimes it seemed a little ironic to me that poor Richard was known as the 'Happy Herbalist'. I'm not denying that he lived a good life and enjoyed it to the full, but was he truly happy?

You'll say it's easy to be wise after the event but somehow I always knew that behind the ebullient behaviour and the ready smile there was a sad herbalist too.

So, I can hear you ask, why did I, one of the world's little people, feel so much empathy with a chap like him, one of life's stars? Why did I enjoy his programmes so much?

Well, the first thing that attracted me was the theme music. You don't happen to know the title and composer I suppose, and whether it is available on record or cassette?

Apart from that I never had the gardening bug. I'd always been more of an armchair gardener but as soon as I heard that theme tune I thought to myself, hello, I bet I'm going to be riveted by this.

Then there was the look of the man and the cut of his jib. Oh, he was a shade tubby, although I hear that television has the unfortunate tendency to make people look heavier than they really are, and perhaps he wasn't so plump off screen, and anyway I understand that many of you women like a man who's got a bit of meat on him.

There were also the jumpers. Did you knit them yourself? Probably not since I hear you are a busy career-woman in your own right. I remember thinking what was so marvellous was the way his jumper always fitted the mood of the particular programme. My own favourite was when he did the programme about knot gardens and wore a jumper with a very eye-catching knot design.

Perhaps you can settle a debating point that was discussed by a few of we gents over a few foaming tankards of best. We all said what a shame it was that he only ever wore each jumper once. What, we asked one another, became of them then? Someone suggested he gave them to charity, but I thought personally that he probably kept them all and wore them about the house. I wonder which of us is right.

Richard also had a lovely speaking voice. I could have listened to him all night coming out with those quotations and Latin names. I have never had the bonus of further education but that does not mean to say I am not partial to a nice bit of literature delivered in a lovely speaking voice.

'I know a bank where the wild thyme blows' – that's what Shakespeare said and thanks to your poor late husband so do I now. Richard's enthusiasm was certainly infectious and I'm currently growing a bit of sage and thyme outside the back door. I tried growing some parsley but that was not a success.

No doubt you have a lovely garden Libby that Richard made for you before his demise. What will you do with it now? Probably you will preserve it as a lovely, natural monument to his memory.

I could go on forever but I know what you're probably thinking. You're probably thinking why does God let people like terrorists and dictators live, yet he takes away poor Richard?

I've had to think long and hard about that one. Perhaps they needed a gardener in heaven. Do you think Richard is in heaven? Or elsewhere? I know you can't believe all you read in the papers but I hear that sometimes he was no better than he ought to be.

Have I said too much? Do I overstep the bounds of formality? I hope not. Words are not my strong suit and whatever Richard's faults let me say that I never objected to paying for my television licence while he was on the box.

Yes, I suppose it's too late to ask for a signed photograph, so since your husband is now tragically dead I wonder if you could send me something a little more personal and substantial. I understand that he wrote some books but I am not the bookish kind so don't bother sending any of them.

Do you know what I'd really like? Yes, you guessed, one of Richard's old jumpers, preferably the one with the knot design. I am not a large chap and would probably find it very roomy but I promise I would cherish it, wear it often, and only wash it gently using biological powder and a fabric softener.

I look forward to hearing from you at your first convenience, and remain yours in a shared loss,

George Woods (bachelor)

'You like the car?'

'Sure.'

'It's a forty-seven Ford Sportsman.'

'You don't say.'

'You want to photograph me standing against it?'

I said I did. We turned off the highway. I set up a few poses. It was your standard rock musician stuff – fancy car and the wide open spaces of America. It was straight out of the Rolling Stone book of rock clichés. Besides, it wasn't easy to keep him interested.

'Bolivia,' he said, 'now there's an interesting country. The value of the illegal cocaine crop is two or three times bigger than the combined income from all the country's other products.'

'You're full of information,' I said.

He was full of something.

I set out the Polaroids on the back seat of the car and watched the fake colors settle, become ethereal, flat yet translucent. Steve Campbell leaned over the side of the car and looked at the pictures I'd taken.

'They're good.'

'They're okay,' I said.

'Guess you've got high standards.'

'That's it.'

He got restless again, jumped behind the wheel and we took off in a flurry of grit and sand. He drove fast and pretty well considering how out of it he was.

'You say Harry protects you.'

'That's it.'

'What does he protect you from?'

'Oh, you know, fans . . . groupies . . .'

This was apparently a joke. He found it pretty funny anyway, and he started laughing very loud. Then he said, apparently seriously, 'No, Harry protects me from *myself.*' But maybe that was a joke too. He started laughing again. I reckoned I'd had as many answers as I was going to get on that subject.

We drove. There was no denying it was fun, the soft-top down, the big engine burbling, some off-the-wall music on the in-car stereo, ('The only thing on the car that isn't original').

When we got back to the Santiago Inn there was a blue pick-up parked out front with Harry sitting at the wheel.

'Uh oh,' Steve Campbell said.

'I don't understand,' I said. 'Does he work for you or do you work for him?'

'That's right. You don't understand.'

'Are you scared or what?'

'You get out now,' he said. 'You'd best take your Polaroids with you.'

'No,' I said. 'You can keep 'em.'

I got out of the car and watched as it headed down the road, slowly this time, followed by Harry in the pick-up. They headed back in the direction of the dirt road that led to the weird house. I'd have given a lot to be a fly on the wall and hear what they said to each other when they got back.

My hotel room was in darkness when I got back. I hadn't opened the blind before going to meet Steve Campbell. The projector was still in position. I opened the blind now. Hot light flooded the room and right away I knew something was wrong. I knew somebody had been in the room and things weren't the way I'd left them.

I opened the drawer in the bedside table. Libby Wisden's check was still there. A swift look through my photographic equipment showed there was nothing missing there either. In fact, shit, there was more than there should have been. In the corner of my gadget bag there was a new camera, a brand new Leica, a sublime piece of equipment that would have cost somebody the earth. I took it out of my bag and saw that it still had what looked like a price tag attached. But it wasn't a price tag. It was a tiny little gift tag and on it was written, 'Sorry. Harry'.

It seemed kind of an excessive way of saying sorry for a smack in the face, but I wasn't complaining. Then it clicked that maybe that wasn't all he was saying sorry for. Then I knew he'd stolen Richard Wisden's transparencies.

I phoned Libby in London and told her the news.

'But you've seen them?' she said.

'Yeah, but only briefly. Do you want to send duplicates?'

'I don't have duplicates.'

'Shit. Do you want me to call the police?'

'I'd rather you didn't.'

'Thing is,' I said, 'I probably know who took 'em.'

I told her about Harry, about Steve Campbell, and about the house in the desert. It meant nothing to her.

I said, 'Why would anybody want to steal those pictures?'

'Because they contain vital information about Richard's death.'

I'd been expecting that.

'Look, Mrs Wisden,' I said, 'I've looked at those transparencies, you've looked at them, and if we're honest we both know there's nothing there. They're just pictures.'

'Surely the fact that this man Harry stole them indicates that there *is* something there.'

'But there's no connection between Harry and your husband.'

115

'Isn't there?'

'Er . . . I don't know. Until this moment I didn't think so. Either way he's welcome to those pictures. I still don't think they mean anything.'

'You're a disappointment to me, Miss Sagendorf.'

'Then have your money back.'

'That won't be necessary.'

She hung up. I felt bad. She wanted me to feel bad and I did. I'd got five thousand dollars from her, some money from Steve Campbell, a new camera from Harry; no wonder I felt bad. I showered. I ate. I watched some television. Then the phone rang.

'Hello.'

'This is Harry.'

I didn't know what an appropriate greeting would have been. I said, 'Can I have my transparencies back?'

He said, 'Sure. I've finished with them. I only wanted to look, that's all.'

'Harry, has anybody ever told you you go about things the wrong way?'

'Yeah, some people told me that.'

'Why'd you want them?'

'I wanted to find out who killed Richard Wisden.'

'Oh, come on.'

'No shit. You want to come over to the house, I'll explain everything.'

Like a fool I promised Harry I'd be right over. Like an even bigger fool I kept my promise.

Libby Wisden handed over a lot of money and I told her about Richard's dream. Being a Piscean he was bound to dream a lot, and dreams can tell us an awful lot about ourselves. He

116

told me about this one dream he'd had a few weeks before he died.

First he was in a helicopter looking down on this desert, and the helicopter kept flying along and there wasn't anything there, just desert. Then suddenly in the distance there was a sort of oasis, like a fertile square marked out in the sand. And when he got closer it was obviously one of his herb gardens, and he was working on a knot garden at the time which is highly significant. There it was miles from anywhere in the middle of the desert, this typical English herb garden with a sundial in the middle. But as he looked down from the helicopter the pattern of the herbs in the square kept changing. So it would start out and it would be a circle in a square, but then the lines of plants would rearrange themselves into letters, into knots, stars and stripes, or swastikas.

Then suddenly he wasn't in the helicopter any more. He was right in the middle of the garden, standing where the sundial had been, but the sundial wasn't there now. Then he wasn't standing any more, he was sitting on a chair and then he realised he was tied to the chair. Then he wasn't sitting there at all. He was suddenly in a hole in the ground, still tied to the chair so he couldn't move, and they were filling up the hole so he was being buried alive. And then he woke up!

Well! There was so much to interpret I didn't know where to start.

First of all the desert. Well that's a bad sign because it shows the dreamer's life is barren. It kind of means death, literally, but also symbolically, like there's a death-wish present, and maybe that was because Richard thought he'd 'dried up', possibly emotionally, possibly creatively but possibly sexually. Perhaps he was scared of impotence. Lots of men are! Or perhaps he *wanted* to be impotent. You'd have to explore the rest of the dream before you could say definitely.

The fact that there's a garden growing in the desert, that's really a hopeful sign. Gardens in dreams can mean all sorts of things, like the desire to bring beauty and peace into your life, a yearning to bring back the past, like a return to Eden. The garden can also express the dreamer's desire to grow – to find new interests, possibly to cultivate new talents.

The *kind* of garden is all-important. The garden wasn't overgrown or anything, not full of weeds or anything like that. It was very orderly and I think that shows the state of Richard's mind, which was very orderly too. It was in distinct shapes and that tells you a lot. I don't want to get technical, but a circle in a square, well, that's very nearly an archetype. It's the process of becoming or giving birth to something new. And the swastika, that represents the ideal man. Of course it's also a knot garden and that's pretty simple. Richard's mind was orderly but it was tied in knots. Not only was his mind all tied up, he was also tied to the chair. That means he felt life was restricting him and holding him back.

All this is reinforced by the sundial. Anything to do with clocks in dreams means a fear of death, a fear that time's running out. Richard must have felt he didn't have enough time left to do all the things he wanted to do. He didn't want to live by the clock. Later the sundial's disappeared and he's at the centre of the garden. It's as though he wants time to obey his body clock.

But then he finds himself in a hole. Where there isn't any sun!! For a gardener that's pretty significant. Holes can mean all sorts of things, like wombs and vaginas and all that, but this is a hole in the earth, mother earth if you like, and that suggests a return to the womb of course. On the other hand you've got to remember this is a hole he doesn't want to be in, and he can't get out and he's having dirt thrown all over him. So I think the hole is probably the rectum and this bit of the dream symbolises fear of homosexuality.

Whatever its absolute meaning the scene of being buried alive is the climax of the dream. This may mean that Richard's life was stifling and suffocating him. It might mean his present life was killing him but that seems a bit too obvious to me. Being buried alive can be an inverted dream about birth. Very few of us can remember our birth, but let's face it, it was bound to be traumatic, and when you're really upset the trauma comes back in the form of a dream, but the birth trauma manifests itself in the form of a dream about death.

So there you have it. That's what I told Libby. She looked

118

at me as though I was some kind of maniac. Richard always said she was supposed to be so bloody smart but I had to spell it all out for her: Richard's life was a desert until he became a gardener but that still wasn't enough. He had other ambitions he wanted to fulfil.

'What other ambitions?' Libby asked.

Well obviously what he wanted was *children*. He was supposed to have had one by this Angelica woman, but he told me he wasn't really sure it was his. And if it *was* his then the poor little sod hadn't exactly turned out to be anything a dad could be proud of.

Richard wanted to be creative in the widest possible sense. He could grow plants and get them to reproduce, but he couldn't have kids himself. I don't mean he couldn't have them biologically. I don't think he was infertile. But the fact was he couldn't find anyone to have children *with*. Libby wouldn't let him lay a finger on her, much less impregnate her, and even though Richard had more than his fair share of sexual partners, none of them was exactly the sort who wanted to be mother to his children.

I told Libby all this. She laughed at me. Cow.

'That's why he died, is it?' she sneered. 'Because he couldn't find anyone to bear him children?'

'That's why he killed himself. Yes.'

All the time we'd been talking, her body language had been very defensive – knees together, folded arms, wearing sunglasses to stop any eye contact.

She said, 'You're an even sillier little trollop than I thought.'

I didn't rise to that. Women like her can say what they like to me. They can't hurt me.

'Who are you to talk to me about children?' she said.

'I'm just me,' I said.

'I find it pretty distasteful when some cheap little tart tells me my husband killed himself because I wouldn't give him children. I find that pretty bloody distasteful.'

I shrugged. She didn't like being shrugged at either.

'It's not me telling you,' I said. 'It's the dream telling you. It's Richard's subconscious telling you.'

She flounced out. I couldn't really blame her. It must piss

you off a bit to realise that some 'cheap little tart' knows your husband a hell of a lot better than you do. Yeah, it must really hurt. And probably I should have been hurt at being called a cheap little tart, but I wasn't. After all, I'm not cheap.

Some actors complain about stage fright. Some call it first-night nerves, but it doesn't only happen on first nights. I know actors who go into cold sweats, throw up or get the runs before they go on stage. Personally I don't have any nerves at all about going on stage and facing an audience. It's just everything else in my life that fills me with complete and utter terror.

That is why I have terrible trouble with auditions. Auditions are real life and they scare the hell out of me. If I had to act I could cope with it. It's when I have to go to an audition as myself that I'm in trouble.

Of course with television it's not actually important whether you can act or not. And if it's a commercial they know all they want to know about you within the first three seconds of you walking into the room. That suits me fine.

They usually use me for something a bit Pickwickian – port, English cheese, margarine with the real taste of the country-side. The fact is I'm short, prematurely bald, and decidedly fat. I didn't choose to be that way. I'd rather be nicely muscled and finely chiselled. I'd rather be juve lead than character, but it's not in my genes.

The thing to keep in mind, however, is that I do actually make a living (of sorts) out of being this size and shape. I know plenty of nicely muscled and finely chiselled actors who made fabulous Mercutios in their end-of-year drama-school productions and who haven't worked much since. All of which proves you don't have to look like Richard Gere for your face to be your fortune, although here I'm using the word fortune in its loosest sense.

One day I got a phone call from a woman I didn't know and had never heard of asking me if I'd be interested in doing some work. This would be like asking Errol Flynn if he was interested in doing some screwing. I said yes before I said anything else.

'Would you like to come over and discuss it with me?' she asked.

That use of the first person wasn't quite right. Directors and agents and casting people always use the royal 'we'. But it would have taken more than that to deter me. I said I'd love to discuss it with her.

'Shall I bring anything?' I said.

'No.'

'Prepared speech or something?' I asked, praying that she'd say no. She said no.

'Tell me,' I said, 'is this for a play or television or film?'

'It's terribly difficult to explain over the phone,' she said. 'I saw your picture in *Spotlight* and you appear to be exactly what I'm looking for. It's a project that is not specifically theatre, television, or film, though it has aspects of all three.'

Oh God. It sounded like performance art. Then I wondered if it was porn. I never thought I had the physique for it, although I did once appear nude in a play about Gilgamesh in a room above a pub in Highgate.

What I really thought was that she was some bored, wealthy housewife who'd been to a creative writing workshop and written a marvellous little play, and hubby was forking out to have it put on in some dubious venue on the fringe of the fringe. There would be talk of transfers and of her many contacts in the world of showbiz. There would be an unplayable script and the offer of a profit share arrangement. There would be no profits.

Still, I wasn't sure enough of all this to stop myself going to talk with this woman. The house was in Hampstead. It was big and modern and crawling with plants and money. I rang the doorbell and a woman answered.

'Hello,' she said. 'I'm Libby Wisden. Please come in.'

121

I could have lived happily in the hall of the house and still had room for a couple of lodgers. Walls and carpet were pale grey. The staircase was open plan, made of light oak, as was the panelled ceiling. There was a narrow marble table by the door, decked out with family photographs. I looked at them and had the first inkling of why I might be there.

She took me into the kitchen. It was full of the smell of fresh coffee. We sat at the breakfast bar. Autumn light flooded in from the garden. There was a photograph album on the bar and Libby Wisden invited me to look through it. It showed Richard Wisden with his family and friends, often mugging for the camera and generally being a clown.

'Are you familiar with my husband's television work?' she asked.

'Of course,' I said. 'Well that is, I've seen a couple of programmes.'

'Has anybody ever commented on the resemblance?'

'Sorry?'

'You do look very much like Richard, don't you think?'

People *had* commented on it. I'd always joked and said I was better looking and I wished I made the sort of money he did. It was true that our appearances were similar – short, fat, and balding; but there's more to resemblance than that.

'Why do I need to resemble your late husband?' I asked. 'Do you want me to play the part of him?'

'I want you to impersonate him.'

'We're not as alike as all that. I don't have a beard. Our skin colouring is different. Our facial expressions . . .'

'The beard can be grown. We can change the skin. We can use make-up.'

'Where and when am I going to be required to do this impersonating?'

'I can't tell you that in case you turn down the part.'

'Our voices aren't very similar, are they? What about our mannerisms?'

I was aware I was doing a rotten audition.

'There will be video tapes to study. You're an actor after all, aren't you?'

I couldn't deny it. It crossed my mind that there could be

an uncompleted television series and they needed me as a stand-in for long shots, something like that. But why was I dealing with the widow instead of the director or producer?

I don't know why, but for some reason I asked, 'Is all this strictly legal?'

She smiled conspiratorially and said, 'How strict *are* you?'

Not very, I had to admit. I studied the photograph albums. It looked like a part I could handle, always assuming I was offered it. Then she held out her hand. It was an elegant and nicely manicured hand, nice enough to have starred in TV commercials, and it was holding out to me a wad of fifty-pound notes. It would pay off my overdraft several times. It looked like I was being offered the job. The sensible part of me wasn't at all sure about this, but somehow the mouth was working on its own and I heard it agreeing to the offer and asking when we started rehearsing.

I was kind of surprised how easy it was to find the track through the desert that led to the house. The 4×4 had plenty of spotlights. It was as good as driving in sunshine. I made out the lights of the house and saw the Ford Sportsman. I could see someone standing on the porch. It was Steve Campbell. He had a guitar strapped on and the lead went through the open window of the house, in to where the amps were. I could hear the sound of harshly amplified power chords. There was no sign of Harry but his pick-up was parked in the back of the house.

I pulled up and shouted hello to Steve Campbell though he most likely couldn't hear me over the guitar. I looked into the house. The main room was in darkness but projected on to one of the walls was the transparency of Richard taking his self-portrait in the mirror.

Campbell stopped playing. The amps still hissed. He set down his guitar. A bass twang reverberated through the speakers. He went into the house and played with some piece of equipment, a drum machine as it turned out, and the heavy electric pounding of a complex synthesised rhythm started up.

I arrived at the house and entered. Steve Campbell nodded at the projected face of Richard Wisden. 'You know him?' he asked.

'I met him once,' I said. 'Where's Harry?'

'He had to slip out. We were the same age, you know.'

'You and Harry?'

'Me and Richard Wisden. Bizarre really. Here I am, into the desert, youth, drug culture, rock, electric guitars. There he is, was, bald, into gardening for Christ's sake, middle-aged before his time. Age doesn't seem to have anything to do with the number of years you've been on the planet.'

'Did you know him?' I asked.

'We went to school together. Yeah, sounds stupid, doesn't it? Same grammar school in Beckenham. That's where David Bowie came from, you know. We all used to hang about in the same pubs. They were called Arts Labs in those days.'

'Harry said he knew something from the pictures.'

'Yeah. He did.'

'Do you know what?'

'Harry's not a good man, you know, not really. He's violent. He has some very nasty friends. Drugs, murder, guns, you name it Harry's into it.'

'And he protects you from yourself.'

'Did I say that?'

'Yes.'

'Must be true then.'

He went over to the projector and changed the slide. The drum machine pounded on. The slide of the Anderson building filled the wall.

'Know anybody called Anderson?' he asked.

I shook my head.

'You're lucky. He's bad news. Harry used to work for him.'

He changed the slide again. This time it was the joke-shop

window. He went close to the image and pointed to a tiny detail in one corner of the display. It was a water-pistol.

'Remember that,' Campbell said. 'That's very important.'

He changed the slide again. This time we saw the interior of the plush living room.

'That carpet,' he said. 'It's Persian. It's an unusual design. It represents a garden. See here in the corners there are hedges formed into knots. This next picture,' and he changed to the pattern laid out in sand on the bare earth, 'shows a pattern that's very similar to the one in the carpet.'

I couldn't see that it was similar at all. I have a trained eye for these things but I didn't think the image of the carpet was clear enough for anybody to make that kind of comment. Then he put up the slide of the naked torso.

'See those veins in the breasts, when the image is enlarged, if you look really, really, carefully, they have a similar pattern, kind of a knot again.'

He stood in the beam of light. The pattern of skin, of light and shade, nipple and vein, shone on his face. The drumming didn't let up.

'That headland,' he said, changing to the picture of the sunset, 'is called Anderson point. This slide of the Italian restaurant, on the wall there's another picture of Anderson point. This wrecked car has poppies growing round it – opium, that's just one of the things Anderson's involved with. Oxford Street, the concrete jungle, that guy on the left of the picture, you can hardly see him, that's Anderson.

'That patio belongs to Richard's house – that's parsley growing there, rosemary, that's for remembrance. The railway lines – lines knotted together. The roofscape – the tiny English houses, TV aerials, radio waves but you can't see those. It's like every TV programme contains clues, messages in the air that are just for you. That's the way it feels if you're a real paranoid schizophrenic, or if you can get hold of the right drugs.'

He flopped down on the couch and laughed fit to bust. I didn't know if he was laughing at me or at his own jokes. He found a bottle of tequila that had been set down by the couch and took a huge swig from it. He offered it to me. I didn't refuse. In the dark, in the middle of the desert, with my ears being beaten up by synthesised drums, being entertained by a loaded English rock musician, I accepted a swig of tequila. It didn't seem like such a big deal.

Steve Campbell said, 'I've told you exactly what Harry would have told you.' Then he laughed some more.

He lifted his feet up on to the couch and in seconds he was asleep. I wasn't going to get any more sense out of him, not now, probably not ever. Where was Harry?

I found the volume control on the amp and turned it down to zero. That was a relief. There wasn't much to do except wait and see if Harry turned up. I took the tequila and sat on the porch. The wood-bodied Ford looked beautiful in the light from the house. I went to admire it and that's when I found Harry.

His body was in a heap under the dashboard. There was some thick liquid smeared over the driver's seat, and Harry's head, big, square and fat, was resting quietly on the back seat.

Dear Libby,

I hope you are keeping well and thanks a million for the letter. More than that, thanks for the package that accompanied it. As I write I am wearing the jumper you sent me and very smart it looks too. The design, embodying as it does, the knot motif will provide me with years of stylish dressing.

As I predicted, it is roomy to say the least, but better that way than the other I think. I have to say that it is not as nicely made and finished off as I had expected but when you only wear things once as Richard Wisden seemed to, quality is perhaps not paramount.

More to the point, you could have knocked me down with a feather when I found £500 wrapped up inside the jumper, especially when you say in your letter that it is mine to keep if only I can tell you how and why Richard died. It is funny you should say that because I have been giving the matter some thought and I have come up with a theory.

You write an interesting letter Libby and you speak truer than you know when you say that Richard didn't kill himself. Take it from me Libby, nobody dies by his own hand. It is always the hand of God. God's finger is always on the trigger. God plants cancers in the lungs of antisocial smokers. Nobody dies without His say so. But it could be I am moving too fast.

First, a confession. I was telling a little fib when I said I was a great fan of your dead husband. It is true that I watched his programmes once in a while but I was not some drooling, uncritical adorer as I implied when my only interest was to get a free jumper out of you. Now the stakes are higher and I must come clean.

Oh television! It is a wonderful thing and it is a terrible thing! It fills me with wonder and it fills me with disgust. There are some very talented people who get on the box – Jonathan Miller and Muriel Gray to name but two. But I think you will agree that Richard was not in their class.

There are also, sad to relate, a lot of people on television who aren't very talented at all. Television, alas, is the medium of mediocrity, and its so-called stars are often as mediocre as the medium. Even if there are one or two who stand out from the crowd they only stand out by virtue of a cheap gimmick – a big bosom, a funny way of waving their hands about, wearing nice jumpers.

People like myself see all these bland no-hopers and these forced eccentrics and we say these television people aren't much cop. They're just mediocre. I could be mediocre too. I could wave my arms about. I could put on Richard Wisden's jumper (I have!) so why aren't I on television?

Perhaps you answer 'no reason at all'. Perhaps you say

it's just being in the right place at the right time and getting the breaks.

So, we're no different. I'm ordinary and these bastards on the television are ordinary as well; but the difference is they're ordinary and they get all the money and fame and sex, whereas I'm ordinary and I get bugger all.

These people are taking what's mine. They take all the money and the attention and the love and I don't get any. This gets me cross, and it gets God cross as well.

Let's look at Richard's case. He seemed a nice enough bloke but you hear things, don't you? He liked a drink. I can tell that from his face. In his books, which I did not find an easy read, he goes on about sex and overindulgence all the time. And no doubt he had a mistress and exotic foreign holidays.

I'm telling you Libby, this sort of thing just isn't on. We all know it isn't on but most of us can't do anything about it. I don't have the sort of personality that would make me a bomb-throwing terrorist or anything like that, so all I can do is watch and pray. And that's what I have been doing Libby.

I went down on my knees and asked God to wipe away the plague that is television. God's answer was a long time coming, and yes I admit there were moments when I doubted Him. I asked God why He had forsaken me. But then Richard died and I knew He *hadn't* forsaken me.

I'm sorry God struck down your husband Libby, but He had to start somewhere. Don't worry. There'll be lots more. God will come sweeping through the programming schedules like a dose of salts and He'll clean out all the newsreaders and the chat-show hosts and the weathermen and the stand-up comedians. They're all for the chop.

So, I hope it is some comfort to you to know why all this is happening. If you want to get in God's good books you should destroy your television, preferably using the purifying agent of fire. You should refrain from sexual activity and dress plainly. Going on your knees before God is certainly worth a try but He's a busy chap and may not have time to listen.

In the meantime please send more money to me at this address, and await further instructions. This is the one true way to ensure salvation.

I look forward to hearing from you again soon, and trust that this will be the start of a beautiful relationship and an ongoing correspondence between us.

Lots of love.

Your friend,

George (Woods)

I went to see a woman called Miss Bogart. She asked me what my name was and I said Trudy, and she asked me what I did for a living and I said I was a working girl, and she raised her eyebrows and said, 'Aren't we all?' So however spiritual she was she obviously had her feet on the ground as well.

The house was one of those big four-storey Victorian places in Earls Court with big bay windows. Most of them have been divided into twenty-seven bedsitters or something but this was divided into four flats and Miss Bogart had the ground floor. It was decorated like a museum, all dark wood with glass cases full of collections of stuff – shells and rocks and butterflies. None of it had seen a duster in years. The lady herself was a bit of a museum piece too. She had grey hair tied in a bun, big yellow teeth and she was wearing all black. I suppose if you're a medium you have to try and look the part.

She showed me into her living room. That had more collections – dolls, fans, animal bones, old photographs. She'd just made some herbal tea and she gave me a cup. I was glad it was only a small cup.

'I sense you have some very specific purpose in coming to see me,' she said.

'Dead right,' I said.

129

'There's someone on the other side with whom you're very keen to renew contact.'

'Yes,' I said. I was impressed.

'I sense there is unfinished business between you and him. Perhaps he died before he had told you something very important. There is something vital left unsaid.'

'That's very close,' I said.

You see it had been worrying me ever since I had that visit from Libby Wisden. I'd been honest with her and told her what I thought was the truth, that Richard killed himself because he was all worn out, tied up, and not able to find a nice woman to have kids with. But she'd left me doubting myself. Perhaps he hadn't killed himself for those reasons. Perhaps he hadn't killed himself at all. I could only think of one way to find out – and that was to ask him.

I wouldn't say I was a big fan of spiritualism, but if there is a life after death, and if you keep your own personality, it only makes sense that the dead would want to talk to us as much as we would want to talk to them. And people like Miss Bogart are there to help the conversation along.

'Did you bring along something belonging to the departed as I asked?'

I gave her a pink water-pistol that Richard had left behind one time. It wasn't much but then we didn't have the kind of relationship where you swap Christmas presents. She took hold of it, and that was it, she was off. I thought at least she'd have drawn the curtains and put on some mood music but no, she sat there in broad daylight and started 'seeing' things.

'I see a rugby ball, an elderly woman called Daisy, a man who played the mouth organ. There's a child who was a great reader. I see gold sandals, a family album with the letter M embossed on the front, someone named Charlie, a crucifix made of mother-of-pearl. Do you have a relative who visited New Zealand? I see a cinema called the Essoldo, a games teacher called Mr Matthews, the name Gulliver, but I don't know if it's a christian name or a surname, a signed cricket bat, a framed picture of Queen Victoria, a bucket and spade, a man with a walrus moustache . . .

'I see a woman with red hair who was very fond of earrings.

I can see one of those globes that are really table lamps. Does the name Mrs Wild mean anything to you? A girl called Karen who died in a boating accident. A man with a withered arm. Identical twins called Eric and, no I can't get the other name. Someone who collected tea-pots. A man with gold teeth. Someone who liked parsley.'

'Yes,' I said. 'That sounds like him.'

A lot of people don't understand how a medium works. A medium is like a radio set. All these messages and signals are sort of floating in the air and the radio has to be tuned to the right station, otherwise it's just a mess of voices and interference. So all these things that Miss Bogart was picking up were messages all right, just not messages intended for me, but if the right person had been there and had been able to tune in they'd have known exactly who Mr Matthews was, for instance.

Actually, I did know someone called Charlie, who'd died of malaria and my sister had one or two nice tea-pots, but she wasn't dead. The parsley was the first thing which sounded spot-on.

'Yes,' Miss Bogart went on, 'he had a taste for parsley. He liked good food generally. He was a little plump, or perhaps just big-boned. He has a beard. He is a kind man, distinguished. Did he have some connection with the land?'

'Gardening.'

'I think he made gardens for people.'

'Right.'

'Could the name be Richard?'

'That's amazing.'

'I see him wearing an unusual sweater.'

'Does he have a message for me?' I asked.

'He says he's very happy on the other side. Life is very pleasant there. He's met up with lots of old friends including his parents. He says everything is very clean and peaceful where he is. The gardens are immaculate. There is no conflict. You shouldn't be afraid of death, he says. It's a gate we all have to pass through.'

'But how did he come to pass through it?'

She closed her eyes and really had to concentrate on that

131

one. Finally she opened her eyes and said, very softly, 'He says it was part of the natural process of spiritual progression.'

'But did he walk through the gate or did someone push him through?'

'He says his time had come and he has left behind all the cares of his previous life. He is so happy where he is now. The sun shines, the food is excellent and there is gentle music playing all the time.'

I was getting excited but also a bit annoyed that Richard was being so evasive. I shouted out, 'Did he kill himself or not?'

There was another long pause with eyes closed.

'He cannot answer that question.'

'Why not?' I asked.

'It often happens that when a spirit passes to a higher plane they can't be bothered with the petty details of the life they've left behind.'

I had to admit that made sense.

'Anything else?' I asked.

'He says he must be going now but he is never far away from you and wishes you good health and prosperity for the future.'

'Say goodbye for me.'

'I see a restaurant, a lady doctor called Temple, a talented young writer whose work is a little too experimental for popular tastes, a joke shop, someone called Harry . . .'

She was off again but it sounded as though her radio wasn't tuned in properly again. None of it meant a thing to me.

When she finished she made some more tea and we both agreed it had been a successful session. She assured me we'd get a lot more out of Richard if we had another session. She talked about poltergeists and about spirits who wake up on the other side but don't like to admit they're dead. It was all very interesting but I wasn't really listening. I was looking around the room at all the masses of stuff – birds' eggs, coronation mugs, pieces of driftwood (in Earls Court?) and loads of books. I even noticed that among the books she had one by Richard called *Grand Designs*. Well, I thought, there's synchronicity for you.

After I'd managed to choke down the last of the tea she showed me out. We were standing on the doorstep and I was thanking her for everything, when she grabbed her forehead and said, 'There's a special message, something specially for you. I'm getting it now. The message is: "Don't go down to the woods today".'

Then she shook me by the hand, closed the door, and I was back out on the street, wondering what on earth the message was all about and what I was supposed to do with it now that I'd got it.

The truth is I never did anything with it. I never even went back to see Miss Bogart. Weeks passed and at first I kept meaning to fix up another session and see if there were any more messages coming through. Then time passed and I thought, what the hell, the message I did get didn't make any sense. When was I ever likely to come across any woods not to go down to? And it certainly didn't get me any nearer to finding out anything about Richard's death.

More than that I'd stopped caring. Richard was dead and that was the end of it in some ways. Libby seemed to want it to be the start of something, some big thrilling action-packed adventure. Why did she want that? I didn't want to go the same way as her. I thought I didn't care. I thought there were more important things to worry about. I thought it was all behind me.

Future events showed how wrong I was and how much I did still care. For a start I got a call from Libby asking me to meet her in room 118 of the Hancock Hotel.

I knew it was insane but I went. Then months later I received an invitation that said,

You are invited to the Regent Room at the Hancock Hotel at 8 p.m. on March 13th when you will learn something to your advantage concerning the death of Richard Wisden.

I knew that was going to be insane as well but I went all the same. Wouldn't you?

As it happens I was a lot smaller than Richard Wisden. I tried on his clothes and found they had a couple of spare inches in all directions. I would have to put on weight for the part. All my life I've dreamed of having to put on weight for a part.

The main problem for an actor who's fat is that too much flesh in the face severely limits its expressive capacity. That's why you see fat actors rolling their eyes, dropping their jaw, and doing all that hammed-up nonsense. They have to do all that before anyone notices that they're trying to convey anything at all.

Richard Wisden was no exception. I sat in his house, in what used to be his study, and I watched endless video tapes of his television shows. He went in for all sorts of mugging and face pulling and generally behaving like a bad actor. All that really says is that he wasn't an actor at all, neither good nor bad, but that he was a 'personality' and that's a horse of a very different shade. He wore silly hats, silly sweaters, made lame jokes, tossed in some pretentious quotations. It was good television.

It meant that he should have been very easy to impersonate. He had lots of quirks that were easy to imitate, and I was perfectly able to imitate them. This meant, however, that I was committing the unforgivable actor's sin of starting from the outside of a part. Libby Wisden was making me spend too much time colouring my hair, getting the walk right, trying on countless pairs of trousers and shoes, when really I wanted to know things like did he vote Conservative, was he kind to his mother, that sort of thing. I tried to get Libby to give me some of this sort of information but it was like pulling teeth.

I'd say, 'Was Richard a good-humoured man?'

134

And she'd come back with, 'What on earth can you mean by that?'

'Well,' I'd soldier on, 'did he worry a lot about things or did he just take life as it comes?'

She'd then say something like, 'It seems to me we have little choice but to take life as it comes.'

In the early days I'd let it drop at that. I didn't want to argue with my director. It never helps. But there came a time when I was getting desperate just to know how the man thought and felt. For example, in one of the programmes he shows the different types of parsley and says, 'Here is God's plenty!' Later he describes angelica as 'the finest plant on God's good earth'. Considering this I thought it might be worth knowing whether or not he believed in God. I asked Libby.

'What an extraordinary question,' she said. 'Why do you want to know that?'

'To get closer to the part.'

'You'll be talking about motivation next.'

'I'd just like to understand Richard. That's all.'

'Why should you when I never did?'

'The more I know, the better job I can do.'

'You have the video tapes. What more can you need?'

'A lot more. Believe me, a lot more.'

That was the end of that conversation.

The other problem was not knowing how or when or for what audience I was going to play the part of Richard Wisden. This was important to me, though not to Libby.

'You see,' I said, trying to sound all sweet reason, 'if, for example, I was going to give a lecture in the character of Richard I would pitch my performance very differently than if I was making a television appearance.'

'Really?' she said, and I could tell she didn't believe me. She thought I was another actor having a queeny fit about his part.

'It's all a question of scale and size and detail,' I went on.

'Is it?'

'Yes. I'm trying to work towards some kind of finished part but I don't know what kind of finish is required.'

'Yes, I see,' she said and she smiled at me in a way that told me that she didn't.

It was nothing new to be involved in a show where nobody knew what they were doing or why they were doing it, or what they were trying to achieve. It's usually called improvisation, but this was worse than usual.

I'd been on the project for a couple of weeks when I got my first suspicion that something a bit sick might be going on. No doubt anybody else would have had their suspicions from the beginning. My hair had been cut and styled. I was growing a beard and I'd put on a little weight. I went to the house every morning, put on Richard Wisden's clothes, watched the video tapes again, walked around, read aloud extracts from his books trying to get the voice right. Libby would watch and give me notes.

'Richard never spoke as quickly as that. He never scratched his nose like that. He never sat in a chair that way.'

It was knackering. It was hard work and it was difficult work, and I'd lost my way in it all. It was only late morning but I'd already had more than enough.

'I'm sorry,' I said. 'I've had it. I don't know what I'm doing. I'm worn out.'

'Would you like a drink?' she asked.

'Great.'

She poured me a glass of claret. She said that's what Richard always drank, not that I cared very much about his personal habits at that moment. She handed me the glass. I took a deep drink and sat back in the armchair with my eyes closed. When I opened them again Libby had dissolved into tears.

'That's perfect,' she said. 'That's exactly the way Richard looked when he sat in that chair, drinking wine from that glass. It's him.'

I knew I'd seen Richard drinking wine on some of the video tapes. The programmes often ended with a shot of him lounging in a deckchair in an English garden, a drink in his hand, watching the sun go down. I'd never rehearsed his way of sitting and drinking but obviously I'd absorbed it unconsciously. I felt rather good about that.

Meanwhile Libby's crying was starting to get out of hand. I tried to console her the way anybody would. I walked over to her chair and put a hand on her shoulder. She launched herself at me, clasped me tight to her and cried and cried into my shirt, Richard's shirt.

'There, there,' I said, or something equally original.

'Oh Richard,' she said. 'Oh Richard, I've really missed you.'

I found that a bit sick.

No way did I ever see myself spending the rest of my life working on the desk in some scumbag place like the Santiago Inn. I was too young. I got too much grief. I was just living cheap, trying to save some money so I could do some of the things I really wanted to do, like travel. I know a lot of people say that doing Europe is really old hat and you should go to South America, but I was never scared of being called old hat.

I'm a great believer in serendipity. You start out looking for one thing, but somewhere along the line you find something else that's more important than the thing you first started looking for. It took me a long time to find anything while I was doing that job.

I told myself when I started that the job would be okay because at least I'd meet people. But who did I meet? Tourists, businessmen, travelling salesmen, other hotel staff, waitresses. I was sharing a room with two of them, real daddy's girls from Palo Alto, finding out what the real world's like before they go home, Daddy buys 'em an Italian sportscar and they do something meaningful like finding a husband. It took me two weeks before I could tell 'em apart. They were always hanging out in the room, in their underwear with personal stereos on, using each other's toothbrush, painting each other's toenails. It was disgusting.

The only interesting person who ever walked into the Santiago Inn, and he was probably only interesting because he'd found the right combination of drugs, was Steve Campbell. He was so right about the Muzak there. It did do bad things to your head. I love music, I really do, anything, Mahler, Chuck Berry, Van Halen, anything. I'd never heard of Steve Campbell and okay, so he was pretty old but he was the most entertainment I'd seen all summer. It wasn't every day someone threatened to whip out his dick to show to the residents.

I'm no groupie or anything but I can see why musicians are so attractive. They're free spirits and they don't punch the clock. They have money and sexy clothes and of course they're creative. The moment he'd gone I wished I'd taken him up on his offer. He offered to give me a tape of his music that I could play instead of the lobby Muzak. The hotel would never have gone along with it but I'd have liked to have it for my own personal use.

As things worked out I got a tape really easily. While Steve Campbell was out with Eva Sagendorf a big guy arrived and said he was looking for him. We got to talking and this guy said he was Steve Campbell's personal manager, so obviously I asked if he had a tape of Steve's music. He did, and he gave it to me.

I know now that the big guy was called Harry and there was all the stuff about him getting murdered, but more about that later. I was so glad to get the tape I couldn't wait to play it.

However, all the time that I was talking with Harry I kept getting phone calls for Eva Sagendorf from someone in England, name of Libby Wisden. I know Miss Sagendorf put through a call to England as soon as she got back, then later that night she went off into the desert again and was gone a long time. Every twenty minutes I'd get a phone call from this Wisden woman in England asking was she back yet, and every time she called she sounded more desperate than the time before.

138

In the end I said, 'Look, I'm only the girl who works on the desk and operates the switchboard sometimes, but, can I be of any help?'

'Only if you can tell me how and why my husband died.'

'Hey, slow down,' I said. 'I can't tell you anything but if you want to talk I can listen.'

Boy did she want to talk. It was real confused, just a mess of names and stuff that I couldn't follow any of, but I kept saying 'yeah' and 'sure' and after about an hour and a half she was sounding a whole lot less desperate.

'If you come up with any ideas, Rosemary,' she said, 'call me on this number.'

I said sure and took down her number, and she seemed a lot happier and I put down the phone. I don't mind dealing with crazies so long as they're on the other end of a phone, and that phone's on the other side of the Atlantic.

So it was late before I got to listen to the tape. My Walkman was nothing special and of course the girls I was sharing with had five-hundred-dollar models so I borrowed one of them. It was lying around and there was nobody to ask so I just borrowed it.

The music was a little flaky. It had a beat and you could have danced to it if you were real energetic. I guess the beat was coming from a drum machine because it sounded synthetic and then there were layers of wailing guitar, but not playing your typical lead guitar solo, just making noise, but pretty exciting noise. Then once in a while there'd be some real loud sound-effect type noises – engines revving, jets taking off, machine-gun fire, bombs exploding. Then on top of all this were the vocals. Sometimes it was singing, Steve Campbell I guess, but sometimes it would be voices from TV and radio, snatches of sentences that kept repeating. It was strange stuff, 'that's for remembrance', 'you understand last night was just a comedy', 'don't go down to the woods today', all kinds of weirdness. You couldn't have mistaken it for the latest Diana Ross album.

I was on my bed listening to the music when suddenly one of the bitches snuck up and grabbed her personal stereo off my head. 'It's manners to ask,' she said. I couldn't believe a remark like that. I had to listen to the rest of the music on my own crappy set.

Next day I got called to the manager's office, could I come right away. I figured she'd made a complaint against me, and when I got to the office there were a couple of police sitting there. It seemed a little out of proportion for borrowing somebody's stuff without their permission. But of course what they really wanted to talk to me about was Harry's death. I was one of the last people to see him alive.

It all sounded so horrible and they demanded I give 'em the tape. I said no way. It was mine. It was a present. Then they asked me disgusting questions about was I having sexual relations with him. I wasn't even sure whether they meant Harry or Steve Campbell. It was so gross. I had to give 'em the tape but they said I'd get it back. If they really thought there was some clue to the murder on that tape then they were *really* grabbing at straws.

They put Steve Campbell under house arrest which I think must mean they never really thought he was the murderer. He couldn't stray far but they let him use the phone, and would you believe it, he called me.

'I'm sorry about all this,' he said.

He had a cute voice, kind of English but not too much.

'All what?' I said. 'You didn't do anything, did you?'

'That's right. Not a thing. Hey, you don't think I killed Harry, do you?'

'Well of course not,' I said, and I really believed what I was saying but I didn't have any reason to believe it.

'How old are you?' he asked.

'I'm nineteen,' I said, but I was adding a couple of years.

'I'm old enough to be your father.'

And *then* some, I thought to myself, but all I said was, 'It's how old you feel that counts.'

Suddenly he said, 'I really love the desert, you know, but they're doing terrible things with it. Nuclear testing. It's underground, but still . . .'

He went into a long rap about nuclear weapons. I heard him say something about people who'd been out in the desert too long starting to glow with radiation. Sure I care about nuclear war, ecology, all that stuff but what can you do about it? You've got other things on your mind, like whether to grow your hair, whether to buy a Toyota, how to lose your virginity. I guess I wasn't absolutely the only virgin in the state of Nevada that year but it sure felt like it.

'You want to come over?' he said.

'How? What do you mean?'

'I can't leave the house but the guys from the local force who are here guarding me, they're nice guys, they've said they wouldn't mind if I had one or two visitors.'

'Oh, I'd really like to but I'm not sure.'

'Come on. You'd make the prisoner very happy. The condemned man always gets his last request.'

I told him I'd have to think it through.

Dear Libby,

I have not heard from you for some time. No doubt my last letter gave you plenty to think about. I hope you have come to terms with the contents of that letter and have started to make your peace with the Godhead.

I hope, for your own sake, that you haven't been watching too much television but if you have you will know that the grim reaping I talked of is taking place in the land of the small screen.

They are dropping like flies and I can't tell you how glad I am that God has pulled His finger out and is doing what I asked Him. Not before time. It gives you a funny feeling to know that God is doing your bidding. It gives you a feeling of power and no mistake.

You won't have noticed Libby but I have been keeping an eye on you. My, but you do dress nicely. In my last letter I told you to lay off the glamour and the old war paint

141

but I take that back now. I usually prefer the natural look rather than a lot of tarting up, but in your case Libby you've improved on nature and that is very acceptable.

I particularly enjoyed the wide-shouldered blue suit with the pencil skirt that you were wearing with the man's shirt and red tie. I also admired the sheer black poncho-styled baby-doll nightdress you had on last Thursday, also the wet-look cache-sexe and the pink high-heeled mules.

Yes, there's no point denying it, I've been taking a peep through your curtains late of an evening. I know you won't mind since you are the uninhibited sort and not hung up about your body like so many females.

I have decided we must be together. We will make a great couple, but that in itself is neither here nor there. The fact is, it's God's will that we should be together and you can't argue with that, can you?

One slight problem is that I'm a good deal older than you but I'm still fit and active and over the last years I've been keeping my body as a temple.

More problematic is that I am a man of limited means and I wouldn't want anyone to think I was just in it for the money since you are fairly rolling in it. I think it would be best if you paid a lump sum into my bank account and we can tell everyone that I have a private income which will then be true of course. I hope you find this acceptable. God and I certainly do.

But hold your horses, I hear you say, who is this man? Who is this George Woods with whom my future is inter-twined?

I am a man Libby, take me for all in all. However it is just possible that you have heard of me. I have never had access to the mass media but plenty of people are familiar with my business. I have premises not a stone's throw from Islington's Upper Street, and my business rejoices in the name of George Woods Fun Emporium. I specialise in harmless, if saucy, fun. Thus: plastic dog and elephant turds, black-face soap, artificial vomit, plastic skulls, mice, rats, and snakes, sweets that make you fart, dribble glasses, chattering false teeth, false beards, indoor fire-

142

works, knives that retract into their handles, arrows through the head, bloody fingers, light switches in the shape of tits, a thousand and one different items in the shape of the phallus, nude playing cards, water-pistols. In short, the lot.

I have never made it on to the small screen but I have provided literally thousands of people with entertainment – the good, old-fashioned kind. I have regular customers from all walks of life. My window displays are well noted and tourists often stop and take snapshots of them.

So you see, I am by no means the nobody you thought I was!

If you know what's good for you, you will call in at my shop on Friday evening at about closing time, i.e. 5.30. I shall close the shop. There will be wine and finger snacks, and on the very floor of my emporium I shall make love to you, roughly but with infinite care. Please come wearing something suitable.

This is the way it was meant to be. God and I put our heads together and decided your husband had to go. In a way I'm sorry, but fear not, we'll both get over it.

If you don't turn up on Friday you'll be sorry. You'll live to regret it but not for long since you'll be as good as dead. This would be a shame for both of us but that's the way God and I want it.

In the meantime I trust you will be sending me lots more money, a photograph of yourself which needless to say I shall regard as a treasure beyond price, and also please an item or two of soiled underwear, preferably flimsy and preferably black with red edging.

I am yours, but you know that already, and on Friday you'll be mine. It sounds good to me.

Yours, more than Platonically,

George

My husband and I moved to a delightful fen village outside Ely in mid 1973. The house was lovely, if a little run down, and came with two greenhouses and three quarters of an acre of rather damp wilderness. Everyone in the area grows things so it only seemed natural to want to start growing things myself. I'd never been a great lover of flowers. Fruit seemed like too much hard work. So I decided to grow herbs. They are hardy if you pick the right ones. They don't take up colossal amounts of room, and they are saleable. Gerald, my husband, rather poo-poohed my profit motive. At that time he had a madly well-paid job in Cambridge with computers, but he died of a heart attack a little over two years after we moved here. He was fifty-five, only a few years older than I. The insurance guaranteed that I would not starve to death but there is more to life than not starving. I was therefore very glad that I had my herb-growing business. It gave me a small income and, just as important, kept me occupied. A garden does not let you sit around brooding. It demands that you do something.

I had begun by growing sage, thymes, fennel and a range of mints. I tried to grow basil but that defeated me for several years, and I moved on to hyssop, rue, rosemary and lemon balm. I began humbly enough selling potted herbs from a roadside stall that I set up by the front gate, with a handbell that people could ring for attention. After Gerald's death I became a little more adventurous and started selling herbs through local shops. However, I continued to work in my garden most days, always hoping that someone would ring the bell and provide a welcome interruption.

That was how I met Richard Wisden. An old yellow van pulled up at the gate one day and the driver rang the handbell

144

for attention. It was Richard. He seemed a very young man to me then, although I suppose he was in his early thirties. He was rather slim then and had most of his hair which he wore long as was the fashion in those days. I saw into the van and noticed a mattress and cooking pots. I later discovered this was what he called home.

He bought a pot of spearmint and we talked for a while. He had enormous charm and I invited him to have tea on the lawn. I was rather desperate for company. He looked as though he hadn't had a good meal in ages and he wolfed down toast, cakes and biscuits. He was very flattering about the house, the garden and my small business. He then said he had a confession to make.

'You see,' he said, 'I had an ulterior motive in coming here. I wasn't just driving past and happened to stop and buy some herbs. I've driven past a few times and every time it's struck me that there's something perfect about this place, and something tells me I belong here.'

I wasn't very sure what he meant, whether he intended to buy me out, or move in, or what. I soon discovered what he had in mind.

'Let me park my van in your drive. Let me work for you. I won't expect paying, just so long as you teach me everything you know about growing herbs.'

I'm sure that if Richard had been anyone other than who he was I would have told him to go away, then called the police. But as I said, he was a man of infinite charm and my business was getting to the stage where I could use another pair of hands. I had employed a few casual helpers from time to time, boys from the village. They had been uniformly unsuccessful and occasionally disastrous. I knew Richard had to be better than them. I agreed to a six-week trial and insisted on giving him meals, even if he continued to live and sleep in his van.

If the circumstances of my meeting with Richard strike an outsider as unlikely, I can only say they seemed no less unlikely to me. However, I have learned that if you are prepared to let unexpected things happen to you, then happen they will. After Gerald's death I was, on the one hand, very closed and rather dead. On the other hand another part of me was crying out for something to happen and change my life.

I will also say that a young man living in a van and wanting to learn about herbs was a lot less curious and alarming in 1976 than it would be today when young men want to live in dockland penthouses and learn all there is to know about merchant banking.

The rest, I suppose, is history. It took a depressingly short time to teach Richard everything I knew about growing herbs, and before long he was starting to teach me. He was taking evening classes. Once in a while he would drive down to London and work in the Chelsea Physic Garden. He read a lot of books and magazines, and pumped dry anyone he met who could tell him more about his subject.

I think he would be the first to admit that he didn't have green fingers. His gifts were as a front man, at making contacts and at marketing. Before long we were selling herbs through florists, health-food shops, garden centres, delicatessens, even through a department store. We had a market stall and we began supplying fresh herbs to local restaurants.

We started to do wonderfully well. It took a little time but not so very much. We started to make money. Richard bought an old caravan which saw him through a very bleak winter. He used that winter to study and to make grand designs for the following year.

He decided to become a garden designer. He saw himself making knot gardens, mazes, parterres. It all sounded rather pie in the sky to me. Where in the whole of East Anglia would you find a customer prepared to employ a garden designer?

London was a different matter. No doubt in London it is easy to find some overpaid barrister or stockbroker or media person, or no doubt a computer person, who finds the idea of paying a couple of thousand pounds to have someone remodel their tiny Fulham garden perfectly sensible. In the country this would be regarded as plain madness.

Richard was not one to be deterred by common sense, although if he was an optimist he was certainly not a dreamer. He had a wonderful head for business. He may have looked

146

rustic and unworldly but when it came to calculating profit margins or driving a hard bargain he had a cool and rather ruthless brain.

I was surprised when Richard announced one day that he had been talking with a businessman in Ely and had struck an agreement for us to build and plant a small knot garden for him; our first. However, I was becoming used to surprises.

We spent a very long time deciding on a design, consulting with the client, buying plants where we couldn't supply them from stock, etc. etc. We gave it more attention than it probably needed or merited, but I was as keen as Richard that our first attempt should be absolutely right. We really did work incredibly hard.

We designed the knot garden, laid it out, planted it, all with enormous diligence and care; and at the end of it all this dreadful man refused to pay us. He said he wasn't satisfied with it. He claimed that it wasn't the way we'd described it to him, that we'd misled him, that some of the plants didn't look very healthy – as if he knew anything at all about plants. And so it went on. In retrospect I think he never intended to pay us at all. He was simply a crook. And of course that kind of bad debt hurt a small firm like ours very badly.

We had several meetings with the man. Richard tended to use charm. I tended to alternate between pleading, and demanding legal redress. They were all equally useless. He was determined he wasn't going to pay.

Then Richard had an idea. He went back to the man and said he was very sorry that things hadn't worked out. He admitted that he might have made a mistake or two, and that the customer was always right. He said he was sure the differences could be resolved if he did a little more work on the garden, and if the client still wasn't happy we'd call it quits and he wouldn't have to pay a penny. The man, obviously thinking we were even bigger fools then he'd first taken us for, readily agreed.

All this sounded out of character for Richard, and I thought he was just pouring good time and money after bad, but I didn't try to stop him.

On the appointed day he set off in the morning to begin the

extra work, and returned at midday looking pleased with himself. 'Hop in the van,' he said. 'I'll show you what I've done.'

We drove to the man's house. The gardens were extensive, and had been beautifully kept; immaculate lawns, trim hedges, gorgeous flowerbeds full of hollyhocks, delphiniums, dianthus and violas. In this setting our knot garden was really quite a small feature.

Richard showed me his morning's work. He had attacked the lawns with engine oil and a rotovator. The hedges had been hacked to pieces. Every flower had been cut down or uprooted, or had weed-killer poured over it. Everywhere things were dying, mutilated, looking burned and yellow. Richard had left the knot garden untouched, a little oasis of order amidst the pillage, a little something to remember him by.

I was terrified. I was sure Richard had broken any number of laws, and even if the police weren't called in, what was to stop this awful man doing the same, or worse, to my own humble plot? But Richard had calculated correctly. The man called on me the next day, while Richard was wisely absent. He was furious and made a variety of threats, but it was obvious that he was a coward and that it was all just words. We had won. At least Richard had.

I confess I thought this man had deserved most of what he got, but I couldn't help feeling sorry for the poor plants. I sometimes feel racked with guilt when I'm pulling up weeds. Who's to say what's a weed and what isn't? The wrecking of a beautiful garden was an act of which I would have been quite incapable. Richard said that the man didn't deserve to have a beautiful garden and I could agree with that. All the same, the murder, that's how it seemed to me, of that number of plants struck me as rather wicked. Richard, I feared, had found it really rather enjoyable.

Libby Wisden said, 'I've been thinking, Paul, about what you were saying about the need to know what kind of performance you're working towards.'

At last, I thought. I've finally made some progress. I've got through to her.

She said, 'I think it's time you gave your first public performance.'

'Great.'

'Something small scale with a very limited audience.'

'That sounds fine,' I said.

You will hardly believe the extent to which it turned out not to be fine.

Ever since the episode with the glass of claret it had been dawning on me that Libby Wisden might be simply insane. Her husband had died; her mind had snapped. She wanted her husband back and was employing me as a replacement. It sounded mad? Well why wouldn't it if the lady was that way herself? I justified my part in the proceedings by telling myself: a) the poor dear needed humouring, b) there was nothing mad about her money, and c) maybe I was wrong. When she said I was about to give my first public performance I thought, well yes, I was wrong, she isn't insane, now we're getting down to business.

The next evening I put on one of Richard Wisden's suits, a charcoal pinstripe, with a yellow bow tie and a fedora. My beard was fully grown by now and I must say I thought I looked the part. I got Richard's car out of the garage. It was an old classic Porsche 911. I'd never driven anything like it and I stalled three times between the house and the first set of traffic lights. Libby was strapped in beside me, all fur and red leather. We made a good-looking couple.

Libby wouldn't tell me where we were going, or what sort of performance was expected of me when I got there. She said she wanted me to be spontaneous. She gave me instructions where to go, when to turn left or right, and before long I saw that we were approaching Paddington. She told me to find a parking space, which was no easy task, but I got one in the end and parked.

We walked a few hundred yards and up ahead I saw a big, old, grey building with the sign Hancock Hotel on it. I never get stage fright but this time I was starting to get nervous.

We walked into the hotel. Libby didn't stop at the reception desk. 'I already have a key,' she said. We travelled by lift to the first floor. The doors opened on to a dingy corridor that led to room 118. We walked down that corridor. Libby slipped her key into the door. I don't know what I was expecting – a corpse, blood stains, the stench of death; but it was an ordinary room – small, depressing and bleak, but perfectly ordinary.

'Sit down on the bed,' Libby said.

I sat. She opened the wardrobe door and got out a suitcase. She took from it a camera, a few small envelopes, a map of Derbyshire, a water-pistol. She set them on the bed. Then she produced a bottle of whisky and a bottle of sleeping pills and placed those on the bedside cabinet. She closed the curtains. She turned on the television set.

'How does it feel?' she asked.

'It feels pretty sick, if you really want to know.'

'I want you to tell me how my husband felt that night when he sat here, either alone or with others, and how he felt about killing himself and how he felt about being killed.'

'How would I know?'

'You're an actor. You've been through it all. You look like Richard and sound like him. You've seen his programmes and read his books, sat in his house, talked with his wife. Tell me what he felt that day when he came here, when he lied to me about going to Derbyshire, those days when he occupied this room. What did he do? What went through his mind?'

'You should know better than me. You lived with him. You married him. I'm just here doing a walk-on.'

150

I reached for the whisky. It was only a prop but the contents were real. I opened it and took a swig. I needed it. Richard Wisden would have needed it too. I knew Libby was watching me but I didn't know if she was watching me as an actor or as a ghost. She was in a state. She was nervous and excited at the same time. She looked as though she was in pain and she also looked as though she might explode. I didn't feel in control of my audience. I suppose that's because it was real life that I was dealing with. Then things started to go *seriously* wrong.

There was a gentle knock on the door and Libby immediately went to answer it. I turned my back to the door but I heard a girl's voice and I heard Libby say, 'Come in, Trudy'. I turned round and saw a small, blonde woman in a very low-cut dress. She looked at me and started to scream. She had amazing projection and she didn't tire easily. I tried to calm her down but that only made her worse. Hotel staff and other guests came running from all directions and somebody said, 'What did he do to you? We'll have him.' I'm sure there must have been occasions when actors have been lynched for their performances, but that's the nearest I've ever come. I got out but I'm not sure how.

Afterwards I wanted to do nothing more than go home to my own grotty flat and wash off the stench of this whole business, but I couldn't because I'd left my house keys in my own clothes back at the Wisden house. I didn't want to go back there but I had no choice, and in any case Libby needed someone to take her home. She was in a mess and I wasn't in such wonderful condition myself. I've done some draining shows in my time but nothing quite like this one.

I accepted when Libby asked me in for a drink. I sat in the chair and emptied a glass several times. Whether I was still in character I couldn't say. I asked Libby who the screamer in the hotel room was and why she'd reacted that way, and how she came to be there, but Libby was almost comatose by now. She crossed the room and sat on the arm of my chair, and, oh shit, put her arms around me and kissed me on the mouth. Then she started to undress me. It didn't seem a lot more insane than anything else I'd been through recently, so I found myself going along with it. I'm not very proud of myself for it but I returned the favour. I started kissing and undressing her. We made love, if that's the word for it, on the floor of the Wisden lounge. I can't say it was the most delicate and skilled bout of lovemaking anyone's ever seen, but by God it was intense.

Later, but not all that much later, I sprawled half on the parquet floor, half on the Persian carpet. Libby was very calm. She nestled against me and said, 'You know, in some ways you're not at all like my husband.'

After I told Steve Campbell I'd have to think about it, about going to visit him at the house, I spent the next twenty-four hours thinking about nothing else.

Would any sane person go visiting a heavy drug-using murder suspect in the middle of the desert? She might if he was as cute as Steve Campbell, and a musician, and if there were going to be a couple of cops there in case things got out of hand. Even then, I don't think I'd have gone if it hadn't been for what happened next with the bitches.

We'd all gone to bed at around midnight but I couldn't sleep. My mind was full of stuff and I just lay there with my eyes open. It was pretty dark but after a while my eyes got used to it and I could see plenty. There was a kind of a buzz coming from one of the beds, but there was nothing unusual about that. It happened most nights when one of the daddy's girls used her vibrator. It usually went on for about fifteen minutes, then I'd hear a big sigh and she'd go to sleep. That all happened more or less as usual but then right after the sigh the one who was in the other bed said, 'My turn now?' and I saw her hand reach out and this big white *thing* was passed from one bed to the other. They didn't even bother to wash it. I was *grossed out.* I wanted to throw up. It gave me plenty to think about. What if they got really horny and out of control one night and decided to pick on me. I didn't want to lose my cherry to a couple of expensive dykes.

Next day I did something about it. I phoned Steve Campbell's number and I spoke to one of the cops and he put Steve on and I said I wanted to come right over but I didn't have a car and I was supposed to be working. He said he could fix something.

An hour later a police car pulled up in front of the Santiago Inn and an officer got out and told the manager I was wanted for more questioning. Well, the manager didn't like people seeing a squad-car on his premises because it was bad for business so he was happy for me to get the hell out of there. Of course the officer in the car, whose name was Chuck, was one of the guys who was supposed to be keeping Steve under house arrest, and it shows how likeable Steve was that he could get the police to act as his chauffeur.

We drove into the desert until we came to this house that was every bit as off-the-wall as Steve's music. Chuck was as nice as could be and told me to run along inside where I'd find Steve. Well, I didn't find Steve and the fact is I didn't want to find him right away. I wanted him to find me. I found the bedroom and I went in and took my clothes off and got between the sheets. I wanted him to find me just like in a movie.

Well, I waited and waited and nothing happened. I could hear voices outside and sometimes footsteps, and once I called out 'Steve' but nobody came. I looked at a pile of books he had beside the bed. It was all heavy stuff – poetry, philosophy, that sort of thing. Then I saw there were some letters there too and I knew it was real wrong of me but I read them. I wished I hadn't. They were weird. They were suicide notes, would you believe. The first one said something about 'drugs are quick', and another said things went wrong too many times, and another said 'last night was only a comedy' which I recognised as a line from Steve's lyrics. But what was weirdest of all was they were addressed to someone called Libby and they were signed by someone called Richard,

153

and that of course tied in with my phone call from the crazy lady in England. Maybe she wasn't so crazy after all.

Then, naturally, just as I was putting the letters back, Steve Campbell had to walk in.

'I'm sorry,' I said, meaning the letters.

'It's not important,' he said.

I gotta say he didn't seem fazed to find me in his bed. He didn't seem too thrilled either. Maybe he was so used to finding chicks in his bed that it didn't turn him on any longer, but I didn't think so. I knew guys. At least I thought I did. At least I was sure I wanted to.

I think he was on something or other. He was talking about nuclear testing again and people glowing and he was talking so fast that you couldn't have followed it even if you'd wanted to. He closed the bedroom door and then he shut the big wooden shutters on the windows so that the room was in almost total darkness. I heard him press some switches on a stereo deck and music started. He said, 'This was my biggest hit.' It was a real song, real conventional after the other stuff I'd heard by him. I liked it but it had a downer lyric about 'Young Suicides'.

I was pretty nervous about being there and being on the point of losing my virginity, but shit, I was looking forward to it as well. I could hear him taking his clothes off. I could hear boots and jeans hitting the floor. I was ready. I was more than ready.

Then I saw something that made me want to die. I didn't believe my eyes. The room was pitch black. I couldn't see Steve's face or body, but there, clear as day, larger than life, very erect, and with a fucking *luminous glow* to it, was a big, disembodied dick moving across the room and heading straight for me.

I screamed, only once but it was pretty loud. I didn't know I could scream that loud. The police officers burst into the room firing warning shots. They turned all the lights on and we saw what the luminous thing was. Steve, for reasons known only to himself, had painted his dick with luminous paint. He thought it was a big joke like his dick was radioactive or something. I couldn't see the joke but the police seemed

154

to think it was hilarious. One of the shots had wrecked the stereo and they were real apologetic about that.

Everybody calmed down and we all had a beer and Steve rolled a few joints and things got a lot mellower, and by the end of the evening I was pretty smashed but at least I'd lost my virginity – to Chuck as a matter of fact. He wasn't a great-looking guy but he seemed to know what he was doing and he made it real easy for me. It was quite a day. Serendipity.

We stayed up all night and I saw the sun rise over the desert. We got through a lot of dope and I was really wasted. I picked up the phone and called Libby Wisden in England. I don't know what time it was there but she answered. She sounded as wasted as I did.

'Cause and effect,' I said. 'That isn't always the answer.'

'Then what is?'

'Serendipity. Maybe. Like maybe your husband took a leap in the dark, like a gesture.'

'Are we talking about existentialism?' she said.

'Well I'm surely not because I don't know what that is, but you know, domino theories, there doesn't have to be a first cause. There doesn't have to be a cause at all.'

'You think perhaps Richard killed himself for no good reason?'

'There aren't good reasons and bad reasons. No reason is as good a reason as any.'

'And if I said I know Richard didn't kill himself?'

'How do you know what you know?'

'I can't say.'

'See what I mean?'

I'm recalling the most coherent part of the conversation. It was all just stoned logic but it must have meant something to her because a few days later I got a cheque from her for a thousand dollars.

I saved the money and it came in real handy. A long time later I got an invitation that read,

You are invited to the Regent Room at the Hancock Hotel at 8 p.m. on March 13th when you will learn something to your advantage concerning the death of Richard Wisden.

155

London didn't seem so far away and I had nothing to keep me where I was, and even though I didn't care two hoots about the death of Richard Wisden, I thought, let's go. I want to go to Europe. I want to take my own leap in the dark. Serendipity.

Dear Libby, (or should I call you faithless Jezebel),
You did not come to my Fun Emporium as God and I had ordained. I was there all spruced up and dressed in my best bib and tucker, hair brushed, all bodily parts free from unsightly odour. There was Tafelwein from more than one country of origin, and there were snacks to tickle even the most jaded palate.

I had planned to give you a quick once round the premises. They are not large but they have many fascinating aspects which I can enliven with a few dry and salty anecdotes.

By then we would barely have been able to keep our hands off each other, try as we might, though personally I would not have been trying very hard. The merest accidental touch, a sidelong glance, a curl of lip, all would inflame our senses and before long we would have dispersed our clothes and have fallen on the floor and each other like a pair of sportive gazelles.

But you did not turn up.

At first I felt sure you were stuck in traffic or perhaps you were coming by tube and there was a person under a train, yet I did not think you were the type to travel by tube. I wondered if I had the date wrong but I perused the photocopy I had taken of my last letter and it revealed I had made no such mistake. It is not in my nature to make such mistakes but I was giving you the benefit of the doubt.

The mistake was therefore yours, unholy vessel! You

have had me for your plaything. You have mocked and abused me, but God is not mocked. I could have been all yours Libby, like John the Baptist was Salome's; but now I feel sickened, downcast, tossed aside like a soiled condom.

Even now I *might* forgive you if you got down on your knees, dressed only in a pair of thigh boots and some elbow-length gloves and really begged for forgiveness, but I'm making no promises, and the ball is very much in your court.

The thing I find harder to forgive is the visit from Vesta Security, whoever they may be. I need hardly tell you that it is a shock to the system to be all wound up awaiting the arrival of the object of desire and to be rudely grounded by the arrival instead of two large, ill-educated men in uniforms a size too large for them, chewing gum and wearing five-o'clock shadows.

They said they had come to discuss security and despite my insistence that I felt perfectly secure in mind, body and spirit they would not take no for an answer and insisted, in their turn, on giving my premises a once-over, as they put it.

Do you know what I found saddest of all? These men's every syllable, every gesture, might have come direct from a television programme. It seemed they had styled themselves on the worst sort of villain in a police drama. I think I no longer have to tell you what God and I think about that and I told them so in no uncertain terms.

You'll hardly believe it but they laughed – like brute beasts. They stole my glasses. Then they began abusing my stock. They picked up water-pistols and brandished them in a suggestive manner, and before I could raise a digit, my shop had been transformed into an anarch's playground of stink bombs, dancing skeletons, clockwork mice, chattering teeth, smoke bombs (for outdoor use only), streamers, cushions making whoopee, all generally creating an ambience of chaos. Alas I was not the man to restore order.

Why? I asked and kept asking. Why were they doing

this? They said they were only obeying orders and I said we all knew where that kind of thing got us, but these men were not intellectuals and it is my opinion that they most likely didn't know where that kind of thing got us.

Trying another tack I asked who was giving them their orders, but they were tight-lipped on that as well. All they would say, as they were leaving (and I think I quote verbatim here), was, 'And if you don't lay off that Wisden bint there'll be a lot worse to come.'

Bint? Lay off? How can I lay off when I have never lain on? Forgive me my little joke Libby, at least it shows I haven't lost my sense of humour, and I do think humour is important in a relationship like ours.

Libby, oh Libby, where have I gone wrong? Have I tried too hard? Moved too fast? Surely not. I have been open and honest from the kick-off and you don't strike me as the sort of woman to be put off by a bit of genuine feeling.

That is why I don't want to believe that a person as lovely all-round as yourself would set uniformed men on poor me. But if not you, who? Please do not let it be that you have found another and he is the sort who sends heavies to beat up his rivals.

Look, seriously, God and I aren't going to take that lying down. Still, on the other hand, I'm not made of wood. I can take a hint and I don't want any more stock ruined.

You may be familiar with that old saw 'Eat, drink and be merry for tomorrow we die.' Shakespeare, I wouldn't be at all surprised. It could have been Richard's motto and it may become yours. The fact is Libby, and I don't want to get too philosophical here, whether you eat, drink and are merry or whether you're an abstemious and miserable old sow, you're still going to die. It may not literally be tomorrow in your case, but when it happens, make no mistake, God and I will be behind it and it will serve you right.

That's about it really. I gave Richard's sweater to the jumble sale. Don't be hurt. It really was a bit too flamboyant for me. The saddest thing of all Libby, is that you and me could have been as Gods. As things stand I'll have to be a God on my own. Still, there are worse things to be.

Yours forever and a day,
George

P.S. I never told you this, but in fact I have a small but significant hump. I hoped it would make no difference to us, and certainly it makes no difference to anything now.

P.P.S. I have just received an invitation to the Hancock Hotel where I will, according to the wording, learn something to my advantage concerning the death of Richard Wisden. The only advantage I wanted was possessing you wholly, but if there's some other advantage to be had, don't worry, I'll be there. Did you send me the invitation? It didn't seem your style but I can only live in hope.

London was the making of Richard. He achieved success swiftly and he appeared to handle it well. He was asked to lay out a walled herb garden belonging to a Kensington restaurant. It was lovely – bay trees in wooden containers, variegated sages, angelica, creeping thymes, lavender. The client was delighted and paid him this time. A couple of commissions for Elizabethan knots followed, each one then spawning more work, and on and on. Richard became in demand. He became fashionable. He was written about in *Vogue*. He was employed by the wealthy and the well-connected, people with more money than sense, some would say, people like actors and pop stars, television people, minor aristocrats with estates to keep up. They liked him and they paid him. They took him for one of their own. He wrote articles. He even wrote one

159

about me saying I taught him all he knew. I was infinitely flattered. Then came the appearances on radio and television programmes, then his own series, the requests to do lectures, the books.

I remained in the fens, growing old as gracefully as I knew how and watching Richard's progress. I wished him all the luck in the world, yet I found the whole thing absurd. Perhaps Richard did too. I hope so. His clients wanted someone who would install them a garden in the same way that an interior decorator might install a new kitchen. The idea that a garden might take years to mature and develop was one that would never have occurred to most of his clients. Richard gave them what they wanted, though to be fair, he was rather good at making them want what *he* wanted.

It has always seemed to me that gardeners ought to be the most flexible of people. They work hand in hand with a nature which sometimes obliges them and sometimes drives them mad with failure and frustration. However, there is no point moaning about one's failures and there is no cause to be hubristic about one's successes. Nature and the gardener are in a partnership, but the sensible gardener knows that he or she is very much the junior partner.

This is where Richard and I essentially disagreed. He enjoyed forcing plants into elaborate patterns, tying them in knots, chopping box into spheres and pyramids. He loved the artificial. I would always quote those lines from Pope about 'the amiable simplicity of unadorned nature' in the Epistle to Burlington. 'In all let nature never be forgot . . . Consult the genius of the place.' Richard never had much time for that sort of thing, despite his love of a good quotation. '*I'm* the genius of the place,' he'd snap.

When he first began to get work in London he rented a tiny room in Wimbledon. If some of his grand clients had seen that and his caravan in my garden they'd have been horrified. But Libby changed all that, of course. She had family money and lots of it. She was in a trendy career herself, and she and Richard must have been one of the most fashionable couples around. They married and bought the house in Hampstead. This was in the days when it didn't seem entirely beyond belief that anyone could afford to live in Hampstead. It was a lovely house – very new, cut into a slope, floor-to-ceiling windows, with a brick lily pond, and naturally a wonderful display of herbs.

Inevitably I saw less and less of Richard, and yes, I missed him. My house and garden seemed lonely. My interest in growing and selling herbs dwindled. It suddenly seemed rather trivial.

I was well aware that while Richard lived in his van and later in his caravan, he was drinking a lot and sometimes he smoked marijuana. Of course all young people smoked 'the weed' in those days so that wasn't very shocking, but I think that when Richard got to London he fell in with a set that was drinking and taking drugs in a much more dramatic and extreme way than he was used to. Richard was not a naive man and I'm sure there was no question of him being led astray, or led anywhere that he didn't want to go, but even so I felt he was being harmed and diminished by the experience.

I was equally aware that Richard had a girlfriend and child tucked away somewhere. He never really talked about them and I was never sure how his marriage to Libby affected that relationship, but I was certainly aware that his son and his former girlfriend didn't seem to share in Richard's success.

I last saw him about a week before his death. He was charming as ever but there was a sadness about him. He seemed full of plans. He wanted to go to Japan. He showed me a book on Japanese dry landscape, which is known as *kare-sanui*, it seems. It was all about Zen Buddhism and contemplation and saying a lot with a little; and it all struck me as totally wrong-headed. The quintessential Zen garden seemed to consist of a lot of raked gravel with a few 'significantly' placed boulders sticking out in what seemed entirely inappropriate places. I said it was all very well but it wasn't gardening. If that was gardening then every labourer who laid a concrete drive was a Zen master. Richard accused me of being flippant.

'I have some wonderful ideas for gardens,' he said. 'If only I could find a client who'd give me my head. I envisage a garden that's a suite of rooms, with high hedges and fences forming the walls of each room. Some of the rooms would be conventionally planted, more or less, with incredibly elaborate knots, some of them so intricate that you might not even be able to see there was a pattern there at all. Some would run wild with poppies and statues made of old bones, others would be raked quartz with one single flowering herb placed asymmetrically. One room will be filled with charred wood, scrap metal and broken glass, one will just be a heap of rotting horse dung.'

When Richard started talking there was little stopping him. I didn't know if he was being entirely serious, but something told me that unfortunately he was. I was starting to think that a great mind, or at least a healthy one, was here o'erthrown. The news of his death came very soon after.

I wrote to Libby to express my sadness but it seemed totally inadequate. However, it was many, many months, at the very end of the summer, before I spoke to her, and then only by phone when she rang me. It was a very odd conversation. She wanted me to identify some poppies that were growing in her garden. Apparently she had found some packets of unlabelled seeds among Richard's personal effects in the hotel room where he died. She had sown them in her garden and they had grown. Now she wanted to know what they were and if Richard might have been trying to tell her something by leaving those particular seeds for her to find. I made as good an identification as I could by telephone. It wasn't so very difficult. From her descriptions I gleaned that they were opium, oriental and corn poppy. I found the whole business inexplicably sad and moving.

Then quite out of the blue Libby said, 'Why did he do it? Why did he kill himself? Did he kill himself? Did somebody murder him? Who? Why? Or was it all a big accident?'

'What can I say?'

'You must have an idea. You taught him all he knew. You're a gardener like he was. Don't tell me you don't have some theory, some solution!'

So, somewhat against my better judgment, I told Libby my thoughts. I told her about Richard's mad plan for a ruined garden. It seemed so negative to me, so destructive, so against nature, that somehow it appeared to me to be a harbinger of death. I told Libby how I wished I had been able to act and try to help Richard. I wished there was something I could have done or said that might have made all the difference, but perhaps he had already been beyond help when he came to me. I felt, hardly for the first time, old and useless.

Two days later I received a rather substantial cheque from Libby Wisden. I couldn't see why she had sent it to me, but I didn't return it. I decided I would use the money to plant fruit trees. I was not sure that was how Richard would have wanted to be remembered. He might have preferred concrete and human sewage, but that was how I wanted to remember him.

I thought that would be the end of my association with Richard and Libby Wisden, and in a way that suited me very well. However, about six months later, the following spring, nearly a year after Richard had died, I received an invitation to the Hancock Hotel where I would supposedly learn something about the death of Richard Wisden that would be to my advantage. I had no desire to gain any advantage but I cared too much about Richard, and was still too upset by his death, to turn down such an invitation.

I woke up next morning and I, Paul Conrad, whoever that is, whatever that name implies, didn't have a clue who I was. It seemed I'd fallen asleep on the living-room floor and now I found myself still on the floor, naked, alone, but wrapped in a sheet which I imagined Libby had thrown over me before going to her bedroom. I had a hangover and I felt like death.

Just as important as not knowing who I was, I didn't have a clue who Libby Wisden thought I was. Did she sleep with me because she thought I was her dead husband? Or just because she found short, fat, balding men irresistible? Or was it just her way of saying thanks for a great performance? Or was she just drunk and it didn't mean anything?

The big issue of who I was didn't get any clearer when I found there was a woman I'd never seen before standing in the doorway and asking, 'Who are you?'

She was a short, plumpish, greyish woman, and she was carrying a doctor's black bag. When I didn't immediately come up with an answer she said, 'The back door was unlocked so I walked in. Where's Libby?'

'In bed, I think.'

She said, 'Fine,' and went upstairs, which I thought was a bit presumptuous. As soon as she'd gone I got dressed. I put Richard Wisden's suit on again and went into the kitchen to make some breakfast. Even from there I could hear raised female voices. The doctor didn't seem to have much of a bedside manner.

I was drinking coffee and eating toast when Libby came down. She was flushed and tousled but she still looked better than most women do even after they've spent an hour making up. She didn't say good morning or any pleasantry like that. She just took some coffee and used it to wash down aspirins. Then the other one marched in.

Libby said, 'I've heard enough, Maureen, more than enough.'

The other woman said, 'You haven't heard anything.'

'That's because you don't say anything I want to hear.'

The dialogue wasn't exactly sparkling and they ignored me completely until the lady doctor turned on me and said, 'And you must be out of your mind, leading her on like this.'

I was speechless. This was real life.

'Leave him out of this!' Libby said.

'It's time to snap out of it, Libby. Pull yourself together and stop playing games.'

Libby said, 'Get out. Get out. I've had enough!' but it was a lot more passionate than it looks on the page. She was close to hysterical and the doctor slapped her across the face, exactly the way they do in movies.

'Hey,' I said. 'I don't think that's necessary.'

'Isn't it?' the doctor said. 'Isn't it?'

I didn't want to argue with a professional.

'All right,' I said. 'If you two want to have a good fight, go ahead. I'll leave you to it. It's none of my business.'

'Isn't it?' the doctor said. 'When you find yourself dying of an overdose, that's when you'll discover how much it's your business.'

Mornings after can always be difficult but this seemed worse than most. I went to Richard's study. I didn't know if we'd be rehearsing or not. I turned on the television and watched a programme about how to cook more exciting offal.

Why was I going to finish up dying of an overdose? I didn't know much about Richard Wisden's death but to me it sounded like it was just an accidental mix of too much drink and too many sleeping pills. It could happen to anyone, but I couldn't see it happening to me. Why should it?

Then the old wheels in the brain started turning and I had a terrifying idea about what Libby Wisden was doing. She wanted me to look like her husband, sound like him, behave like him. Maybe what she really wanted was for me to kill myself like him, then I'd really have got to the centre of the part, and she'd be there asking me how it felt and why I was doing it and maybe then she thought she'd know all about her husband's death. I made up my mind that this was one show that didn't have to go on.

I went into the bathroom and shaved off my beard. It wasn't much but it was a start. I put my own clothes on. As I walked past the kitchen door on my way out of the house I could see Libby was crying and the doctor had her arms around her.

'Men,' the doctor was saying. 'As if men weren't bad enough you had to choose an actor. What next?'

I didn't want to hear any more. I wandered into Hampstead village, bought a newspaper and a packet of cigarettes. I wandered over the heath filling my lungs alternately with fresh air and poisonous fumes.

This'll teach me to accept non-Equity contracts, I thought.

At last I went back to my flat. There was some post, the most pressing of which was a script from my agent. It was a play called *If You Go Down to the Woods Today*, a comedy thriller. It was written by someone I'd never heard of. It had five speaking parts and mine was the smallest – Eric the gay antique dealer who dies after eating poisoned mushrooms at the end of the first act. I spent the evening reading the play. It was rubbish. The gardener did it.

Next morning I rang my agent and said, 'Darling, I'd love to do the play.'

Like so many things I get involved with that play never happened. I'm sure it was no great loss to the English stage but it did mean that I had a long spell out of work. I tried to keep busy but I didn't find it easy. I enjoy working and I don't find it easy to amuse myself. Then I got the invitation:

You are invited to the Regent Room at the Hancock Hotel at 8 p.m. on March 13th when you will learn something to your advantage concerning the death of Richard Wisden.

I didn't think that it would be entertaining exactly but I hoped it might be a nice piece of theatre.

I never went home to Derbyshire and my mother. I didn't really mind. I saw her once or twice and I missed her sometimes but not all that much, not as much as I missed my dad.

I got sent to a thing they called a foster home. It's just like an ordinary house, really. There was a married couple and they were called Eric and Edie and they had three kids of their own and they were all right if you like that sort of thing, but I didn't. At least they were normal. The house was a semi and there was a garage and a hatchback and a garden with a lawn and a swing.

166

And of course I had to go to school which I didn't like. They said I'd fallen behind and I had to have extra practice at reading and writing. They gave me a book called *The Happy Herbalist* which had pictures of my dad in it.

It wasn't too bad a life, a bit boring but I didn't mind that. I thought about my dad a lot and once in a while I had a dream about him still being alive, but I never told anybody about that.

The family I was living with, the man was supposed to be a businessman, whatever that is. He always had piles of business magazines around. They looked boring and didn't have many pictures but sometimes they had a colour picture on the front, and that's how I worked out what I had to do.

The picture on the front of one of the magazines was of the man who used to come to Woodbine Cottage, the one who Libby had shown me a picture of, and he was standing in front of a big building that had his name on it. The name was Anderson. Eric saw me looking at the picture and he was amazed whenever he saw me taking an interest in anything, and obviously he wanted to encourage me so he said he worked just round the corner from the Anderson building. Then I got tricky. I said I'd really like to see where Eric worked. He thought this was progress, so at half-term he took me into work with him and showed me round the office.

It wasn't long before Eric got called away and I managed to slip out – out of the office and out of the building. I wandered the streets till I came to this Anderson place.

I was dressed up all smart and nobody seemed to mind when I walked into the building and I could probably have wandered around all day but I didn't have time for that. I went to the reception desk and told them I wanted to see Anderson.

'I'm sure you'll understand that Sir Leonard is a very busy man. Can I be any help?'

I told her not to be silly. Of course she couldn't.

'Just tell him that David Wisden is here.'

It took a while and I had to go through a lot of unimportant people but eventually I got shown into Anderson's office. It was big. I suppose some people would be impressed by it.

167

'Hello, young man,' he said, all formal and polite. 'Can I offer you a drink? I think we might be able to organise some orange juice for you.'

I said all right. He talked to some secretary and said it would arrive in a second. He was pretending he'd never seen me before. He was a cool customer all right. The orange juice arrived and I hoped it wasn't drugged. He said he'd join me and poured himself some alcohol.

'What can I do for you, sir?' he said.

I didn't like being called sir.

'You can answer some questions,' I said.

He looked the sort of man who wasn't used to giving straight answers, but I had to try.

'Why did you used to come to our house?' I asked.

'Sorry. Which house is that?'

'Woodbine Cottage.'

'I don't believe I ever came there.'

'Yes you did. To collect money from my mother.'

'And your mother is called?'

'Angelica. Don't pretend you don't know.'

'I assure you I'm not pretending. I don't know you, your house or your mother.'

'Then why did you agree to see me?'

'I thought it was quite ingenious of a young boy to march up to the front desk and ask to see me. I assumed it was some sort of school project.'

'Then how did I recognise you from that picture that Libby Wisden had?'

'Libby Wisden? Picture? Sounds like a case of mistaken identity, wouldn't you say?'

'Then what about Johnny Fantham?'

'Fantham?'

'Why did he take me from the hospital and why was he bringing me to see you?'

'I can't imagine why this man, whoever he is, would want to take you from hospital. I can't imagine why he said he was bringing you to see me. But I can assure you I knew nothing about it.'

'Then what about this secret society?'

'Which particular society would that be? Freemasons? The Rotary Club?'

'I don't know.'

'Ah.'

'They have water-pistols.'

'Water-pistols?'

He started to laugh. It was a really nasty laugh. I'd been on the wrong end of that kind of laugh before. I should have got used to it by now, but I hadn't. I felt really stupid. I started to cry.

'Come on, old chap,' he said. 'It can't be as bad as all that.'

'Yes it can,' I said.

He came round the desk and put his hand on my shoulder. He thought he was being like a father. His hand was big and white and disgusting. I pulled away.

'Tell me your troubles, old man,' he said. 'Let's see if we can't help a little.'

'It's my dad,' I said. 'He's dead.'

'And you miss him.'

'Yes.'

'That's perfectly natural.'

'I know that,' I said. 'Being dead is natural as well. I'm just not sure if he died naturally.'

'Oh,' said Anderson, and he went for a stroll around his office.

'You killed him, didn't you?' I said.

He gave me another laugh like he wanted me to feel stupid but it didn't work this time.

'If you think I killed your father then you really ought to go to the police, didn't you?'

'All coppers are bastards,' I said.

'You may well have a point there. But why would anyone kill your father?'

'Because there are bad people in the world. Evil people. Like you. I know the police won't do anything. I know I can't do much. I just think you ought to know that there's at least one person who knows what you are and isn't scared of you just because you have a big office and get your name on buildings.'

169

'I never imagined anybody was scared of me,' he said, but I knew he was lying.

That was the end of the questioning, really. It wasn't a great success. I don't know why I went to see him. I thought he might confess if he saw me, the victim's son, but I never really expected him to. Then I thought he might pull a gun on me and take me down to the basement and torture me. But he didn't do that. He offered me a big white hanky and told me to keep it. He shoved a twenty-pound note into my pocket. He got one of the girls to take me to the canteen for a piece of chocolate cake. Then I was put in a taxi and sent back to Eric's office, even though it was only round the corner.

Eric was a bit angry but he tried to understand. Eric would. Obviously I didn't tell him about Anderson. I told him I'd gone for a walk and got lost. I don't think he believed me, but what could he do? I turned on the waterworks again and Eric put his arm round me.

'You're such a baby sometimes,' he said. 'When are you going to grow up?'

'Never, if I can help it,' I said.

But when I got home there was a letter for me that had been delivered by hand and it had this funny card inside and it was inviting me to some place called the Hancock Hotel where I'd learn 'something to my advantage' about my dad's death. It felt quite grown up getting that. I didn't tell Eric and Edie about it but I knew I'd get there on the 13th and nothing they could do could possibly stop me.

The city is London and it is spring. On the streets there are bare legs and arms. There are also fur coats. There is fast-food litter. Outside a department store a man with a trumpet

170

but without legs plays 'My Funny Valentine'. He is no Miles Davis. Paths cross. Routes intersect. The rubbing of shoulders, bad temper, signs – push, pull, 'fashion sweaters', 'quality products', 'suicide sale'.

The gardens are full of daffodils, crocuses, tulips, grape hyacinths. The earth is warming. Seedlings push through the soil. But not here.

I walk these streets, see these shop windows, collide with consumers. I am seeking a purchase. There is a message for me. It will be made plain in a gesture, the turn of a head, the gentle raising of a plucked eyebrow, a configuration of pedestrians and traffic, of architecture and decoration. Perhaps it is just one word, rosebud. Or a sentence, 'Have you tried this brand?' A man will sit beside me on a park bench and take my briefcase, leaving his own. But I do not carry a briefcase. Perhaps it will be a street sign, the name of a café, words on a tee-shirt, the winner of a horse race, a florist's window that waxes eloquently in the language of flowers, a crossword puzzle, 'The finest herbs reveal a lady' – Esther, 'The woman in Nevada' – Eva.

I walk these streets. What I am really looking for is inspiration. In my pocket is a letter from a woman I do not know and have not met. It is a commission. She has read my work. She has found it elegant, fresh, elegiac, lucid. She is a widow. Her husband has been dead a year and she still has not put him to rest. She still grieves. She seeks the consolations of art, the familiar aura of fiction. And who better than I? Could I, would I be able to, is the sum enough (it is), she knows that writers cannot write to a timetable, but even so might I not possibly write something about the death of her husband? She is tired of 'information', of facts that lead only to other facts, of characters who dance like boxers too afraid of counterpunches ever to square up to each other. She needs Art. She writes a good letter. She signs a good cheque.

So I walk these streets, seeking a point of view, an opening paragraph, an open-ended structure, and yet I need more than this.

She lives in her house in Hampstead. She moves from room

171

to room. She straightens a cushion. She pours herself another drink. She tries on her latest dress.

He lies in the ground. Or was he cremated? The dead man, the late husband. How long was he kept on ice? The subject of the inquest, a joint beneath the pathologist's knife, a legal technicality for the coroner, a headache in the police files, an absence, a hollow. Now, inert but organic, he returns to earth and completes the circle.

I walk these streets. Sometimes I sit in my room. I face the wall. I face the empty page. I too face the hollowness and the absence. In the spring garden things are coming into being, but not here.

Death wears many masks. It has many faces. I do not know the face of my employer. I would not recognise her if she walked into the room. Would she recognise me? Perhaps we would look through each other. One day we shall all be invisible men.

There is a woman on a beach. She feels the wind on her bare arms, feels it pulling her long skirt tight against her thighs. She is an artist, though you wouldn't know it. She gathers shells, pebbles, driftwood, seaweed. She will return to her studio, set down her finds, arrange them into a pleasing composition. Only then can they be drawn. Nature brought to the dissection room.

We send out explorers. They return full of tall tales. They carry back diamonds, rare flora, the bones of mythical beasts. We set their treasures on our mantelpieces. We need to live with just a touch of the wilderness.

In my rented room there is furniture that I do not own, a bed that many have slept in before me. There is pattern everywhere, on walls, curtains, carpets, counterpane. Sometimes I lie alone in bed, a cigarette in my hand, and through half-closed eyes I discern other, more personal patterns. I see faces in the wallpaper, the shapes of animals, bridges, alien landscapes. Very like a whale.

Is any of this consoling? It is afternoon. The sky is bright and metallic blue. I sit at my desk with a blank piece of paper. I see the colours of the distant roofs as the sun slices through cloud. The day is warm, but no warmth reaches this room. I

172

see the chimneys and the aerials. There are messages in the air.

Does Libby want to hear any of this? Or does she want action, glamour, local colour? Perhaps she wants plot, characters boldly drawn. A man and daughter say farewell in a station cafeteria. At an East European toll bridge a white van is riddled with machine-gun fire. The doors of the van fall open to reveal a cache of AK-47s. A man is found murdered in a locked room. A girl dies in a casualty department before a doctor can see her. True love blossoms in the ghetto.

Perhaps she wants answers, the unravelling of the mystery, the tightening of the noose around the villain's neck. If so she has come to the wrong man, but presumably she knows this. I deal in less tangible currencies – an unexplained fragrance in the breakfast room, an ice cube melting on a sun-drenched patio, a shadow falling across the water of a swimming pool.

Money moves. It glides along the usual channels. It passes from hand to hand, greasing palms and lining pockets. Growth stagnates, output falls. There are closures and falling dollars, deficits, buy-outs, high costs of borrowing; but at the close of trade there is still profit-taking, there are victors in the trade war. It is all business as usual.

She wears her money easily (I imagine). It suits her. It hugs her figure, flattering the soft, winning curves in which we can read profit and loss.

There are lights on in the house but the curtains are open. The night is cold blue. The interiors are warm with earth tones. Forbidden glimpses. What the butler saw.

I went to the cuttings library. I talked to people by phone. 'Hello, you don't know me but I'm writing an avant-garde meditation on nature and death, inspired (loosely) by the death of Richard Wisden. I wonder if you'd mind answering a few questions.'

Yes, they would mind. They don't know me and don't want to. They have nothing to say, or whatever they did have to say they have already said several times, to police and doctors and private investigators, even to Libby herself, if only she'd listen.

Curtains close, all except one, a basement window – a

sparsely furnished room, lined with tongue and groove panelling, a stone floor. A man sits on a chair, clearly visible from the
street. He is naked and lashed to the chair with black rope. His
body is grey suet against his bonds. The tying is expert. The
knots are large, neat and immovable. It is a skilled job, one done
for money, not just for fun. Whose money? Whose idea of fun?
He is gagged but he is not blindfolded. He can see his own
humiliation. He is a happy man.

There is nothing more natural than perversion. Uniforms
and high heels, latex and rubber remould our shapes. We are
born again, recarved in our own favourite images, sculptures
in flesh, highly accessorised. We become smooth and cold.
To touch us is to touch metal. We smell of nothing human.
We smell of rubber and leather and death.

I picture Libby, calm with mania, trying to behave naturally,
making no sudden moves, making appointments, trying new
restaurants. Ordinary behaviour. No suspicious circumstances.

The house is still and silent. The television set is unplugged.
There is no sound of bird or beast, nor of water reshaping its
riverbed, nor of earth settling to fill the holes of eye sockets
and mouths, the spaces between ribs.

Soon I shall call Libby Wisden. I shall tell her I have
accomplished something. I can send it to her or I can deliver
it in person. I picture her lean hands touching my manuscript
only by its edges.

I shall tell her there are more questions than answers, that
sometimes the answer we find does not fit the question we
first asked. I shall tell her not to expect too much, to hope
for nothing. I shall tell her that death is her ally, the only one
she can finally rely on. I shall tell her that bondage equipment
is as natural as garden flowers.

I walk these streets. In my pocket is a black-edged invitation. There is room at the feast, empty chairs at a late
supper. I do not know my host. Regrets only. I'll be there. I
wouldn't miss it for the world. I shall be expecting revelation
and the unexpected. And what else? Catharsis? Solutions? A
sense of an ending? A triumph for the old order? Let us not
aim too high. Let us not expect miracles.

Let us be perfectly clear about this. There is no connection between myself and the other characters in this tragic and sorry tale.

My name is Sir Leonard Anderson. It is not a household name nor would I wish it to be, yet there are a great many households in the United Kingdom and around the world who have a lot to thank my companies for.

I have nothing to hide. There are no undeclared interests. My dealings in property development, import and export, telecommunications, pharmaceuticals, transportation and the entertainment industry are well known and fully documented. I have fingers in many pies but my hands are clean. I certainly know nothing about illegal currency transactions, flags of convenience and soviet AK-47 assault rifles.

I did not know Richard Wisden except as a television personality, although I am given to believe that he attended a party at my home in Derbyshire, Redlands, in the late seventies. My guest lists in those days were extremely diverse. By no means was everyone who attended a friend. Some were complete strangers. Such was the case with Richard Wisden.

It is true that shortly before his death I discussed with Richard Wisden the possibility of employing him to redesign a portion of the gardens at Redlands, but his plans proved grossly unsatisfactory and I did not proceed with the matter.

It is also true that Swallow Properties, a wholly owned subsidiary of Anderson Holdings, owns the freehold on a Derbyshire property called Woodbine Cottage. This was acquired as an insignificant part of a much larger deal involving building land adjacent to some of my own property. Because of planning difficulties the site has remained undeveloped,

175

but there is nothing sinister about this. Nobody was more surprised than I to discover that the tenant of Woodbine Cottage is the mother of Richard Wisden's illegitimate son. I can assure you this is entirely coincidental. Until very recently I had never set eyes on this lady or her son. Suggestions that I was a caller at the cottage, that I had an affair with the lady, and indeed that I am the father of her child strike me as laughable, not to say insane.

I had a meeting with the boy, David, in my office some while ago. At that time I was entirely unaware that his father was Richard Wisden. He seemed a somewhat curious boy but not without charm. He was still clearly very upset by the death of his father and I did what little I could to console him.

Since that meeting I have spoken with trustees of the Anderson Trust, a charitable foundation established by my grandfather Arnold Villers-Anderson, and the trust has informed me that an application from David for a grant to be used towards special education or educational travel would be looked on most favourably.

Between 1978 and 1986 I made a series of ex-gratia payments to Mr Harry Stein of Nevada. These payments came from my own pocket and are unconnected with my business affairs. They were in lieu of Mr Stein's continued services 'minding' Mr Steven Campbell. Mr Campbell was an acquaintance of mine through his professional association with Armalite Records and Armalite Publishing, both wholly owned subsidiaries of Anderson Holdings, which released, published and continues to own copyright on Mr Campbell's earlier successful music.

Although outside my personal tastes, I have every reason to believe in Mr Campbell's talents and abilities, though I concede that in recent times those talents and abilities have been submerged beneath drug abuse and mental instability. For obvious reasons I am unable to comment on Mr Stein's death at this time, but, if as seems likely, Mr Campbell was responsible one can only express one's profoundest regret.

It is indeed true that Anderson Holdings have a controlling interest in a group of twelve hotels, formerly known as the Regency Group. The Hancock Hotel is part of that group. I understand that Mr John Fantham was employed as head of security at that hotel. I have never met the man but I am told by the management that his abduction of the child from hospital was entirely out of character and a blot on an otherwise flawless career. It is my personal belief that there must have been extreme extenuating circumstances and I regret that these did not come out in court. But let me stress that I have no personal interest in the case and speak only as a disinterested observer.

It is indeed true that I am a friend of Mr Basil Shaw, but our relationship is a social and not a business one. It has been suggested that it was on my recommendation that Mr Shaw made a series of unsecured loans to Richard Wisden. You will agree that since I did not know Richard Wisden I would be unlikely to make such a recommendation. I also feel sure that Mr Shaw needs no help from me in judging the wisdom or otherwise of making unsecured loans.

I have consulted my diaries and it appears that between November 1982 and April 1984 I attended three social occasions at Mr Shaw's house. To my knowledge Richard Wisden was not in attendance on any of those occasions. If drugs were taken I remained unaware of it. If sexual intercourse took place between any of the guests, either on the premises or later elsewhere, I should not be so very surprised. That is what tends to happen at parties, but I certainly witnessed nothing that could be described as an orgy, and I would most certainly not have participated if such an event had occurred.

I know nothing about any secret clubs to which Mr Shaw may or may not belong, and I am certainly not a member of any such. I have never heard of the Posthumous Society and cannot imagine what they get up to with toy water-pistols.

As far as I can recall Trudy was in attendance at only the last of Mr Shaw's parties which I attended. We exchanged the usual sort of conversation. I would most strongly resist any suggestion that she was then, or at any other time, working as a prostitute.

Of course it is true that Anderson Holdings owns the mews

177

cottage in which Trudy lives rent free, but this should surprise nobody. She is my daughter after all.

It is true that Vesta Security is a wholly owned subsidiary of Anderson Holdings, but it goes without saying that that organisation has never been involved with illegal activities, be they threatening the welfare of children or wrecking retail premises. Anyone making such accusations will rapidly find themselves having to substantiate them in a court of law.

I married my second wife, Dr Maureen Temple, in April 1976. My wife retained her own name throughout the marriage. Sadly our marriage lasted only two years before ending in a divorce that, however regrettable, was at least amicable. I am told that she was briefly Richard Wisden's GP and is now a close personal friend of Libby Wisden, but that friendship only began after our divorce.

My second wife and I enjoyed entirely normal marital relations, in the true sense of the word. I thoroughly resent any slurs suggesting sexual incompatibility, and will not add credence to those slurs by bothering to deny them.

Trudy, to keep the record straight, was the child by my first wife who died in a point-to-point accident in the early seventies.

I met Mrs Libby Wisden for the first time about one month ago. I found her a charming woman, though obviously overwrought, and in the course of our meeting she offered me a sum of money which she somehow imagined would induce me to reveal something or other about her husband's death. I need hardly say that I turned down the offer.

I understand that Mrs Wisden is now receiving expert counselling. I am sure this is for the best and I wish her a speedy recovery. But in conclusion I can only repeat what I said to her: I know nothing, absolutely nothing about the death of Richard Wisden.

You're probably wondering why I asked you all to come here to the Regent Room of the Hancock Hotel, hardly one of London's finest hotels and I apologise for that, but since it was the scene of the so-called crime, I could think of nowhere more appropriate.

I would like to thank you all very much for coming. There are, alas, one or two noticeable absentees – John Fantham, former employee of this hotel is, I'm afraid, now detained at Her Majesty's pleasure. Harry Stein too, I'm sure, would have been delighted to be here had he lived. And I'm sure you'll all be as sorry as I am to hear that Libby has today been admitted to hospital to receive the very best medical and psychiatric treatment. Her attempts to unravel the so-called mystery have resulted in a certain amount of unravelling of her reason. I'm sure you'd want to join with me in wishing her a speedy recovery. To the rest of you – Dr Temple, Dan Rowntree, David, Basil Shaw, Ms Sagendorf, Trudy, George Woods, Paul Conrad, Rosemary, Esther, my friend the author, Sir Leonard – the very warmest of welcomes.

I hope you'll forgive some of the more melodramatic touches accompanying this meeting – black-edged invitations delivered by special courier, the elaborate precautions to make sure you came alone and were not followed, the fact that we meet in this soundproof, locked room, the fact that you were searched for weapons and bugging devices. You will soon see why these precautions were necessary and I am grateful that you submitted to these small indignities.

I said you would learn something to your advantage and I don't think I've misled you. Tonight you will learn the truth about Richard Wisden's so-called suicide in room 118 of this hotel. The truth will set you free. I hope you'll all find that advantageous.

First you will need to know who I am and how I am able to speak with such authority. That much is easy. Perhaps some of you know already. I am Richard Wisden. I see that is a shock to some of you. I'm well aware that I don't look or sound like my old self. The plastic surgery was a lengthy business but a complete success, as you see. I have changed the style and colour of my hair, transformed my accent and speech patterns, my style of dress. I have lost a good deal of weight. I am a new man. Some would say I'm unrecognisable. In some ways I hope so.

One or two of you may find this hard to believe. You may think I'm not Richard Wisden at all, but an actor, or some strange employee of Libby, or perhaps you think I'm a charlatan and a madman. I think I can change your minds. I *am* Richard Wisden. Please trust me and listen to what I have to say.

I hope the seats are comfortable. I trust you all have drinks. I now face the hardest part of all, and that's knowing where to begin. Conan Doyle says 'Detection is, or ought to be, an exact science'. I do enjoy a good quotation, though it seems to us now that detection is merely a minor form of semiotics. However, you will not deny that the notion that crimes can be solved by detection is a very optimistic one. It shows that we believe in the primacy of reason, the triumph of good and the restoration of order, although I know it can sound a little right-wing when you put it like that. I shall try to remain liberal.

First, since I am standing here before you it is clear that I did not kill myself in this hotel, and certainly I was not murdered. There was a dead man in my bed. He was an actor. He was rather good but good actors are ten a penny. I paid him well and he worked very hard on his performance, just as Paul Conrad would work on his. I told him I needed a double for a stunt I wanted to perform at a charity dinner. He was a convincing performer and no less a convincing corpse when I killed him. Libby was convinced he was me.

But it possibly started before then. I had already planted a

180

few clues with the contents of the suitcase. They were perhaps a little prosaic, a little plodding, the map, the camera, the water-pistol, the seeds. All red herrings yet all convincingly symbolic.

I paid a hotel maid to plant the key to the boot of my hired car in room 118 after the police had searched it. I wanted John Fantham to find it. I wanted him to go to Derbyshire and find the suicide notes. Being a rather unliterary soul Fantham didn't realise that the letters were imitations of famous literary suicide notes. Of course if the letters had fallen into the hands of, say, Dan Rowntree, this might have been known earlier, but I'm not sure what Rowntree could have done with that knowledge.

I subsequently employed Vesta Security to put an abrupt end to Mr Fantham's investigations. He, Mr Fantham, was also instructed that part of the price for the safe conduct of his daughter was that he should free my son David from hospital. I thought that David, obsessed as he seemed to be with adventure stories, guns and car chases, might find the whole thing very exciting and I'm sure he did. David is much more intelligent than most people realise. His escape from Fantham was marvellously clever. It was probably just as well that he did escape. No doubt Anderson would have got the shock of his life to have David delivered to his front door.

My various instructions to Vesta Security and via them to John Fantham were conveyed by telephone since by then I was in Nevada, living under an alias and heavily disguised. There I intercepted the thirteen slides that Libby had sent to Eva Sagendorf and replaced them with thirteen others that I had picked at random from my own collection before disappearing. The fact that some sort of narrative or solution could be read from those images didn't surprise me in the least, but it wasn't of my making.

Over the years I've seen Steve Campbell decline from a talented musician into a drug-dependent wreck. We've known each other since school and while I haven't been the friend I'd have liked to have been, I did what I could for him when I got to Nevada.

I was horrified at what I saw, and that's why I got rid of

Harry Stein, because he wasn't protecting Steve. Harry was the one keeping him hooked. I had no qualms about it. Stein was a bad man. He worked for Anderson, didn't he?

It was I who suggested that Steve Campbell daub his penis with luminous paint, although he never knew it was Richard Wisden who suggested it. He hadn't seen me for years and my disguise was heavy. I do a very passable impersonation of an American cop. Steve Campbell knew me as Chuck, and Rosemary from the Sàntiago Inn knew me even better. Defloration hasn't ever been one of my particular enthusiasms but I was happy to be of service.

Trudy, I feel, has been badly used in all this, but you might say that's inevitable in her chosen profession. I had her running round the country in a hired car, taking photographs of her father's gardens; but perhaps I was most unfair in telling her my so-called dreams. I invented a dream world which presented my subconscious in a suicidal state and I told it all to Trudy. I knew she'd attempt to interpret and make sense of it all.

I was aware that Trudy knew a medium called Miss Bogart. I approached the good woman, this time disguised as a Scottish wine importer, and by the simple act of giving her a lot of money, arranged for Trudy to receive the message, 'Don't go down to the woods today'.

I thought that phrase had a certain resonance. I gave the boy in the car-hire firm a tee-shirt with those words on it. The woods are an emblem of intrigue, mystery and threat, Dantesque if your mind runs that way, full of evil spirits and toadstools, and of course I knew Trudy had a client called George Woods.

I'd known about his Fun Emporium for years, though I'd never visited it until after my so-called death. Disguised as a Canadian tourist I paid him a visit. Then by paying him enough money I drew him into my plans. I told George to write to Libby. I told him what to write and when to send the letters and when to organise the little wine and cheese evening that Libby was destined not to attend. I'm afraid I was also responsible for his shop getting wrecked by Vesta Security.

While on the subject of 'don't go down to the woods today',

I was the one who suggested the line to Steve Campbell for use in his music; and I was the one who approached Paul Conrad's agent with the play of that title. I posed as a producer and insisted that she send it to him immediately. The play was actually written by the same young author who was commissioned by Libby to write a so-called fiction about my demise. He had written the play some years earlier and it showed none of the avant-gardism with which he subsequently made his small but significant reputation. The title had to be changed and didn't have much to do with the play, but more about him later.

The employment of Dan Rowntree to exert his objective critical faculties on my collected writings was one of the more unpredictable aspects of the plan. I knew he would grasp the literary allusions and I naturally never expected him to enjoy my work, and I didn't think he'd be overly convinced by my glimpse of the heart of darkness. Even so, I never envisaged that he'd lose all sense of proportion just because I had tupped his white ewe. It made for unforeseen complications but I welcomed those.

I have always taken pride in my writing. I even, you guessed, wrote that piece of avant-gardism that Libby commissioned from the 'promising young writer'. The writer was real enough and was delighted to be paid by Libby. I understand he doesn't get paid very often for his writing. But he was even more pleased when I paid him again and handed him a manuscript that he presented to Libby as his own work.

Basil Shaw and I go back a long way and he was responsible for some of my early success. He gave me a loan when every bank in England, or so it seemed, had turned me down. The truth is that he didn't invite me to join the Posthumous Society. I invited him. Certainly he stamped his own banker's personality on it, but it existed long before he was a member. That was why I got the loans. I offered to take him along to a party if he let me have the money. He did, of course.

Whether you think there was anything sinister about the Posthumous Society depends on whether you think there's anything sinister about orgiastic sex. Personally I don't, but either way there's nothing like a secret organisation for muddying the waters of detection.

I have much to thank Esther for. Shortly before my so-called death I described to her an anarchic knot garden made of waste material. She saw this as unnatural and abhorrent. What she didn't realise, what nobody seemed to realise, was that I did complete such a knot. I completed two. The first was made at Woodbine Cottage. The garden there is a wasteland – scrap metal, broken glass, bricks and smashed concrete, old sinks and pipes, a broken fridge, car tyres, exhausts, filthy rags, dead sparrows, even some weeds. There's a garden for you to contemplate.

Angelica never saw it. She never saw what I was doing. She never saw much. I suppose I must have loved her once. I certainly loved my son and continue to. I have no doubt that he is my son, and nobody else's.

What is Sir Leonard Anderson's part in all this? Why do so many signs point in his direction? Answer: because I wanted them to. I wanted Libby to believe, or at least suspect, that he'd murdered me. And why did I want that? Because I knew that Libby and Anderson had been conducting an affair behind my back. A romantic entanglement. I wanted them punished for that. I didn't care how much distress Libby was caused. I didn't care if Anderson was falsely accused. Why should I? They were only getting what they deserved.

I look around the room and I see lots of blank faces. I see some disbelieving stares. Perhaps I have said too much, or perhaps you think I've said nothing at all. No doubt you will see flaws in my logic, inconsistencies in my so-called motivation, missing links, gaps in credibility you could drive a bus through. You may see things that you think don't *tie in*. So what?

The biggest question you'll be asking yourself is: How did I know what Libby would do following my death? How did I know she would approach John Fantham, or her GP, or go to see David, or give my writings to Dan Rowntree, or ask Esther to identify the poppies, employ Paul Conrad, etc. etc. etc.?

Quite simply because I told her to. There was a letter. It

wasn't a suicide note, quite the reverse. I'm afraid I can't quote it word for word but it said that if I was found dead in room 118 of the Hancock Hotel then I had been murdered and there were certain steps she should take to find the killer. I said these steps might seem strange, unlikely, confusing, but if she followed them she would solve the so-called mystery. And Libby, to her infinite credit, and somewhat to my surprise, did exactly as I had asked. She obeyed me after death in a way she never had while I was alive. Perhaps she had a guilty conscience. Perhaps she genuinely wanted to know who had murdered me.

Inevitably not every single thing happened exactly as planned. I didn't know, for example, that Dr Temple had designs on Libby, and certainly I had no plans for my own son to be shot in the leg, nor indeed that he should go to a foster home. But beyond a certain point of intention, or causality, it really didn't matter any more. Every complication, every coincidence, every intertwining, served my purpose. The only question that now needs answering is: What was my purpose?

That's easy. I wanted to make another knot. The first was at Woodbine Cottage. The second was a more ambitious work.

I have always enjoyed tampering with nature, be it to cultivate plants that would not normally grow in the English climate, or making geometric designs in herb gardens, or clipping hedges into shapes not found in nature.

The garden, however, is a limited form. I wanted another sort of knot. There is a wilderness out there that we tame and convert into 'manageable' gardens laid to lawn with tasteful arrangements of shrubs and hardy annuals. This is madness! Nature knows no taste. It is not neat and manageable. It is not about English gardens, gentle lupins and tall hollyhocks. Nature is a motherfucker. And I wanted to embrace her.

Death is a part of the process, not a very difficult part. The actor I killed in the hotel room, the decapitation of Harry, they were so easy. The difficult thing is to make it mean something. So I drew my outlines, sowed the seeds, waited for the knots to form. Gradually the knots tightened. They

185

spelled disorder. They meant nothing, but the mind does not allow meaninglessness. My death became a Rorschach test in which others saw what they were predisposed to see.

I wanted them to see the world for what it is – a set of misleading clues, a burned-out maze, a noose. I wanted them to feel the noose tightening. I wanted them to recognise the knot in their heads as well as round their throats.

Libby seems to have recognised it better than any of you. She has been driven to distraction trying to unpick the knot. Her mind is disordered. At last she is in touch with nature.

So there you have it. End of story. Mystery solved. I hope I've left you with a satisfying sense of an ending. Of course I may have succeeded only in leaving you with the impression that I am a raving lunatic, that I am not Richard Wisden, that he died in this hotel, that he was murdered or committed suicide, that I have invented everything and solved nothing. Perhaps you think the real solution still lies elsewhere. But your uncertainties only make my knot more elaborate and splendid.

Finally I am reminded of those lines of Shakespeare from Macbeth, 'Confusion now hath made his masterpiece'. I may not have made a masterpiece, but I've done my best.

ERIC KRAFT

HERB 'N' LORNA

A Love Story by Eric Kraft

'One all-American joyride of a novel. It held me in its thrall . . .
Eric Kraft is nothing short of brilliant'

Armistead Maupin

'Fans of Kraft will send up a cheer at their hero's rollicking,
fond story about his grandparents and their secret passion . . .
He keeps Herb 'n' Lorna at the heart of his wise and humorous,
affectionate and witty novel'

Publishers Weekly

'This very funny novel – as graceful, complicated and exhilarating as a quadrille – is an appreciation of folly . . . It is all about
sex, and sex, in HERB 'N' LORNA, means everything in life
that is good – craft and art and imagination and hard work and
humour and friendship and skill and curiosity and loyalty and
love. Eric Kraft is an exacting comic novelist whose work is
happy and expansive'

The New York Times Book Review

'The kind of sweetness and passion and laughter Kraft draws
from these ordinary lives is rare and endearing. HERB 'N'
LORNA is the happiest of books – not to mention the sexiest'

The Washington Post

'A whimsical investigation into the past. An exhilarating comic
novel that is both marvellously sly and enormously good-
natured. A wonderful love story . . . but there is much more to
it than that. Loony and beguiling'

San Francisco Chronicle

sceptre

DAVID FREEMAN

A HOLLYWOOD EDUCATION

'This is one book in a thousand, this is the very best of its kind'
Los Angeles Times

'When I say A HOLLYWOOD EDUCATION is the best book anybody has written about Hollywood, *ever*, better than anyone else's book, it's not empty rhetoric. This book is a knockout. It's amazing. It's profound. It's cruel and kind and records things about the movie business – directly and indirectly – that have never been put into print before'
Los Angeles Times

'Once in a while a work of fiction emerges that seems to catch that peculiar addictive madness that is the movie industry. The latest is David Freeman's fine collection of short stories'
San Francisco Chronicle

'Captures the hilarity, the absurdity, and the sadness that range from the Hills of Beverly to the hellholes of Hollywood Boulevard'
Stephen Bach

'This highly readable series of linked stories takes us among the studios, lunch-tables and other battlegrounds where the gladiators of the film world meet'
The Guardian

'His characters have the vibrancy of Damon Runyon's finest creations and the gutter morals of *Wall Street*'s Gordon Gekko'
Today

'A real writer'
Time Out

AIDAN MATHEWS

ADVENTURES IN A
BATHYSCOPE

'This is indeed an exhilarating collection . . . One of the
characteristics of the bathyscope is that it illuminates the
hidden, and Mathews' powers of observation are masterly, his
prose pellucid and revealing, his imagery exquisitely accurate.
The stylistic range is impressive, moving easily from dark
tragedy to metaphysical comedy'
The Times Literary Supplement

'Set variously in an Irish church, along a California freeway, in
an English village, on a Greek isle and in Nagasaki on the
morning of August 9, 1945, these rare and wondrous stories
remind us of how the best Irish writing – like any art – is
universal'
The Irish Press

'A conjuror with words, dealing us fourteen stories in which
jokers, queens and tragic spades are shuffled in hypnotic
succession'
The List

'Splendidly odd and oddly moving stories, the produce of a
unique talent . . . A very exciting debut
John Banville

sceptre

Current and forthcoming titles from Sceptre

ERIC KRAFT

HERB 'N' LORNA

DAVID FREEMAN

A HOLLYWOOD EDUCATION

AIDAN MATHEWS

ADVENTURES IN A BATHYSCOPE

MARK OLDHAM

NEW VALUES

BOOKS OF DISTINCTION